THE DEVIL'S WORK

Marshal Rance Toller is locking up a pair of troublemakers when Angie Sutter, a homesteader from a nearby valley, arrives with the news that her husband was murdered that morning. Whilst Rance has qualms about heading out into the frozen wasteland, leaving only an ageing deputy to stand guard, he accompanies Angie to her cabin — to find not only Jacob Sutter's body, but also that of his neighbour, slain by the same weapon. Meanwhile, back at the jailhouse, the deputy is dead and the prisoners gone . . .

Books by Paul Bedford
in the Linford Western Library:

BLOOD ON THE LAND

PAUL BEDFORD

THE DEVIL'S WORK

Complete and Unabridged

LINFORD
Leicester

First published in Great Britain in 2013 by
Robert Hale Limited
London

First Linford Edition
published 2015
by arrangement with
Robert Hale Limited
London

A catalogue record for this book is available
from the British Library.

ISBN 978–1–4448–2318–9

Published by
F. A. Thorpe (Publishing)
Anstey, Leicestershire

Set by Words & Graphics Ltd.
Anstey, Leicestershire
Printed and bound in Great Britain by
T. J. International Ltd., Padstow, Cornwall

This book is printed on acid-free paper

Books should be returned or renewed by the last
date above. Renew by phone **03000 41 31 31** or
online *www.kent.gov.uk/libs*

AL

1

Chet Barclay sniffed the air apprehensively as he eased out of his cabin on to the hard-packed snow. Propelled by some mysterious urge, he had ventured across that threshold countless times in the previous twenty-four hours. The biting cold tore at his nostrils as he carefully scrutinized the desolate terrain. The landscape was gripped tight in the dead hand of the December Solstice, and yet it wasn't the appalling chill that disturbed him. Any damned fool who chose to winter in Dakota Territory had better expect hardship. No, something other than the cold was gnawing at him!

Squinting against the snow glare, Chet shuffled off to his left, around the side of the log cabin. Before him lay the stables housing his all-important livestock. Although not a man given to introspection, it occurred to him that a Spencer Repeating Carbine was a strange choice of companion for the mundane tasks awaiting him in there. Yet the sense of unease that assailed him was so intense that he found himself abruptly retracting the hammer. After years of living alone, he was reconciled to solitude, yet at that moment the homesteader would have given anything for some companionship.

An icy gust swept around the rear of his cabin, buffeting him and vainly searching for chinks in his heavy buffalo hide coat. The barn beckoned, offering a modicum of shelter. Yet, strangely, he was reluctant to enter. Dark and suddenly forbidding in the weak winter light, the familiar building only added to his sense of unease. Someone or something was on his land. He knew it for a certainty, and in the open he could at least hope to see them coming.

The .50 calibre soft lead bullet

punched down into Chet's left cheek-bone and then shattered his lower jaw, before finally embedding itself in his right shoulder. Its crushing momentum smashed him on to the virgin snow. Gagging on blood and teeth, his carbine discarded and forgotten, he desperately tried to claw his way towards the barn. From inside came the whinnying of startled and troubled animals. A second bullet slammed into his lower back. Jerking under the impact he tried to cry out, but only a bloody froth emanated from his chapped lips. Gradually and irrevocably life ebbed away, and with it went any chance of discovering the identity of his deadly assailant.

* * *

Angie Sutter watched apprehensively as her husband prowled the frozen barren ground in front of their cabin. Such was the temperature that she really should have kept the window shutter tightly barred. Yet the overwhelming anxiety that had driven him to such manic activity had given her the jitters. Never had she seen him in such a state. At well over six feet tall and massively built, Jacob normally enjoyed a calm and placid disposition. Such an agreeable nature had all changed the previous night.

In the dead of winter, and with their chores completed, there had been little to do other than retire to bed. Keen to put down roots and make a life for themselves, the young couple were eagerly trying for a child. As the fire receded in the stone chimney, passions mounted on the straw mattress. The sudden pounding on the cabin's only door had rendered them immobile with shock. Angie's ardent caresses abruptly forgotten, Jacob had finally lumbered to his feet. Reaching for his old Henry rifle he had bellowed out, 'Who's out there? Account for yourself, damn you, or I'll surely fire!'

The silence that greeted such a

forthright challenge was unnerving. Finally, after some anxious deliberation, Jacob had unbarred the door and poked his gun muzzle out. A biting north wind swept into the cabin's single room. Crouching on the bed, Angie had shivered with both cold and fear.

'Show yourself,' demanded her husband addressing the apparently empty blackness beyond. The complete lack of any response was far more terrifying than the sudden appearance of some intruder could ever have been. Finally Jacob had reluctantly closed and barred the door. Nothing more was heard from their mysterious visitor that night, but neither of them had enjoyed the blissful solace of sleep.

*　*　*

Morning had brought with it a weak sunlight, which had little effect on the awful chill. To Angie's appraising eye, Jacob appeared afflicted by a sheer dread that far outweighed the effect of the previous night's disturbance. It was as though he was a party to some terrible secret from which she was excluded. Briefly she wondered if their situation had any connection to the solitary stranger who had approached her husband near the lake some days before. He had been dressed in black from head to foot and even at a distance appeared vaguely menacing. Afterwards Jacob had seemed preoccupied, but flatly refused to discuss the matter.

Angie's recall of that event ended abruptly when her husband bleakly reported a complete lack of any footprints in the day old snow that blanketed the whole valley. That seemed to unhinge something in his mind, because he then flatly refused to return indoors. Muttering vague imprecations, he chose instead to pace up and down outside the cabin, all the time fingering the trigger of his weapon.

'Jacob, please come in,' pleaded Angie again. 'No good can come of this.'

6

Something in her voice brought him to a halt. Turning to face her, his haunted eyes settled on hers. He opened his mouth as though to speak. An unseen force abruptly launched him towards her. A gobbet of blood flew from his lips. The muted boom of a distant gunshot shattered the silence as it echoed around the valley. Despite his bulk, Jacob could not resist the projectile's momentum. Falling full length, he came to rest directly before her. Released from his dying grip, the Henry had landed at her feet. Instinctively she crouched down to pick it up. Blood stained the snow next to her husband's head and pumped from the terrible wound in his back. His body twitched uncontrollably in its death throes.

A woman of weaker disposition would have collapsed at his side, perhaps stroking his face and sobbing in vain over their shocking loss. For Angie such gestures could wait. Tucking the rifle into her shoulder, she aimed down the valley and squeezed off a shot. She recognized it as being a futile gesture, but the noise and recoil made her feel less vulnerable. And somehow she just knew that only Jacob was meant to die that morning. As the sulphurous smell of black powder smoke wafted into her nostrils, she vowed that there would be a reckoning for the death of the fine man lying before her.

2

How anyone could embark on a momentous drunk in such weather, was completely beyond his comprehension.

'Doesn't that idiot know it's likely going to hit fifteen below tonight?'

His deputy merely shrugged. His mild reaction hinted that he too fancied the prospect of alcoholic oblivion. Grunting with distaste, Rance reached for his sawn off. Carrying that fearful weapon with him at all times was a rule he had made long before and never broke. Town drunk or road agent, the magnitude of the arrest made no difference to his state of readiness.

'I'll handle it,' he continued evenly. 'You just keep that stove going.'

'Sure thing, Marshal.'

His elderly subordinate's relief was obvious, and in truth Rance was glad to get some air. Due to their regular diet of steak and beans, the flatulent atmosphere in the jailhouse had been growing decidedly unpleasant.

The barfly who had brought news of the disturbance had made himself scarce, but it mattered not. Marshal Rance Toller knew exactly where he was going. The town of Devil's Lake boasted only two saloons. Solid citizens favoured the Starr, whilst those of a more dissolute nature headed for Pearsall's Emporium. Overly painted Dutch gals and dubious card games only seemed to add to its attraction. Rance permitted it a loose rein, understanding that it allowed the rougher elements the chance to blow off a head of steam. He drew the line at drunken gunplay.

Winter's icy tentacles seized him the moment he stepped on to the board-walk. Street lighting was non-existent, so he stood motionless for a few moments. As his eyes adjusted to the gloom, he scrutinized his surroundings vigilantly. Such care had been learned fast and had stayed with him through the years. Resisting the temptation to pull up his collar, Rance strode swiftly through the slush that covered the town's only main thoroughfare. As always he took the shortest route across open ground. From Pearsall's there came a loud detonation followed by a scream and the sound of breaking glass. He defied the urges of his impatient temperament. A novice lawman might have rushed through the main entrance and very probably found himself in a world of hurt.

Slipping down an alleyway, he entered the rear of the saloon. As expected the storeroom was empty and little warmer than the street. A single oil lamp flickered in the corner. Moving carefully over to an inner door, the marshal gently eased it open. He was greeted by a blaze of light and a heady mixture of gunsmoke and urine. Unnoticed by the room's mostly frightened occupants he carefully surveyed the scene.

Unsurprisingly, a dishevelled oaf waving a revolver held centre stage. He was unacceptably drunk. Overturned chairs and shards of glass covered the floor around him. All the other revellers were keeping well clear of the unshaven, wild-eyed brute, as he was quite clearly a danger to nearly everyone in the room. It was this particular realization that probably saved Rance's life.

A heavyset character in a black frock coat was the only occupant of the saloon to appear completely unthreatened by the ruckus. Securely seated, with a cynical half smile playing on his features, he calmly observed the pantomime playing out before him as he nursed a shot of whiskey. To the town marshal's experienced eye he appeared to be the more dangerous of the two by far. So his course of action was now quite clear.

As the drunk lurched over to the bar intent on a refill, Rance made his move. Transferring the shotgun to his left hand, he drew a Remington 1875

Model revolver and then reversed it so that he was holding it by the barrel. Whilst the majority of citizens of the United States favoured one of the many revolvers on offer from Colt, the marshal had a particular reason for choosing the Remington. The earlier cap and ball Colts suffered from frame weakness, and if employed as a club could bend so badly as to be unusable. Such shortcomings could taint a man's perception of the newer models. The Remington had no such history and with its solid frame, entirely suited the needs of a man in his profession.

Drawing in a deep breath, he burst through the rear door and made straight for the trouble causer. That individual was far too inebriated to register the sudden activity behind him. He just happened to glance in the mirror behind the bar and caught a brief glimpse of the revolver butt as it descended on his skull. Using that same mirror as a guide, Rance holstered the Remington and swivelled a rapid 180 degrees. Behind him there was a heavy thump as his victim slumped to the floor.

Gripping the twelve gauge, he retracted both hammers and pointed the fearsome weapon directly at the man in the frock coat. As the twin muzzles lined up on that individual's face he exhibited a brief jolt of shock and for the first time Rance took a good look at him. Dark brooding features were topped by prematurely grey hair. He was probably around forty but looked older. The harsh realities of life were etched deeply into his pitted face. Recovering swiftly from the unexpected turn of events, those features now relaxed as he in turn appraised his captor. His hard eyes took in the badge pinned to Rance's jacket.

'Very neatly done, Marshal,' he commented softly. 'But why the big gun? That fellow is nothing to me.'

'Mister, you and I both know that that's a damn lie. Now slowly unbuckle your gunbelt and place it on that table.'

For a few seconds the other man made no move. Then a slight smile crept on to his face. It entirely failed to reach his eyes and was completely bereft of humour. Rance felt a chill spread over him. He had encountered enough killers in his time to sense that he was in the company of a very dangerous individual.

'I won't tell you again. Unbuckle, or face the consequences.'

As though growing suddenly bored by events, the gunnie emitted a slight sigh and complied. Rance kept his scatter-gun trained, as he used his left hand to rapidly scoop up the belt containing an 1873 single action Colt Army revolver.

'Now, pick up your *compadre* and carry him over to the jailhouse.'

His prisoner appeared about to protest, but thought better of it. Shaking his head in apparent disbelief, he rose up out of his chair, heaved the unconscious man over his shoulder and headed for the door. The ease with which he accomplished this showed him to be a man of uncommon strength. Following him out, Rance called back over his shoulder to the barkeep, 'Tot up the damage before I release them, Jed. And keep it realistic!'

If the lawman had troubled to look back, he would have seen more than just habitual resignation on the saloon-keeper's face. For once in his grubby existence, Jed was displaying genuine emotion: fear.

* * *

The jailhouse had received a new visitor by the time Rance returned, a highly attractive one, going by the name of Angie Sutter. Sitting quietly in the corner, her drab bulky clothes could not entirely hide a young and shapely figure, neither of which was enough to unduly distract the marshal from his prime concern of locking up the two prisoners. Devil's Lake was a small town; therefore the jailhouse was a small structure. The only cell was at the back of the marshal's office, in full view of any officials or visitors. It was not an ideal arrangement. Privacy was non-existent, but since most inmates were just one-nighters sleeping off a skinful it served well enough.

His deputy's eyes boggled at the arrival of two prisoners, one carrying the other. Rance kept his gaze firmly fixed on the gunman.

'Search them both, Clem. And keep out of my line of fire.'

His assistant appeared bemused at the fuss made over a couple of drunks, but clambered from his chair to comply. The man in the black frock coat dumped his still unconscious burden on a cot, before raising both arms out to the side. He stood motionless, eyes down, as Clem frisked him. Something about his very presence made Rance's flesh crawl, and he did not feel any better when his deputy discovered a cut-down Colt Navy

Sheriff tucked away in a shoulder holster. A cap and ball revolver, it was awkward to reload, but made a good hold out weapon.

'You're packing a lot of iron, mister,' commented Rance flatly. 'You must think Devil's Lake's a real dangerous town.'

'It pays to be careful, Marshal. I might have to demonstrate the benefits of that to you one day!'

Something popped in Rance's head. He had just been threatened in his own office.

'All right, just what is your name?'

Completely ignoring the deputy now patting his legs, the other man favoured his captor with another cold smile.

'My name's my business. You've got no call to lock me up and you certainly can't charge me with anything.'

He had a point, but Rance wasn't finished yet. Something about the man had set his teeth on edge and he didn't much enjoy the feeling.

'Maybe so, but you don't walk away

from here until I get a name. Who knows, there might even be some papers out on you. Oh, and don't even bother thinking about waving any greenbacks under my nose. I run an honest jail here!'

With Clem out of the way, he slammed the cell door shut and turned the key. His body seethed with unaccustomed anger. He wanted to hit something, anything. Unfortunately he couldn't, because his office was full of people. Taking a deep breath, Rance tested the lock on the door. Only then did he ease the hammers down on his shotgun. Replacing it on the gun rack, he finally turned his attention to the young lady. She had remained seated in the corner. Her eyes were red rimmed, either from the cold or from shedding tears. She had fine sandy hair and apparently good teeth. Her once flawless skin was just beginning to show the punishing effects of a northern winter. Gloved hands tightly gripped a Henry rifle and her demeanour hinted at an inner turmoil. With a sigh he sat down on the edge of his desk. It was shaping up to be one of those nights!

'I'm Rance Toller, the town marshal, ma'am. What can I do for you?'

The young lady trembled but said nothing, as though the original disclosure of her name to Clem had been sufficient. Gesturing to his deputy for a cup of coffee, Rance tried again.

'It's hellish cold to be out travelling, especially alone. People usually come to me if they have a problem. Do you have a problem, ma'am?'

Her pale troubled eyes settled on his as she finally spoke.

'My husband is dead.'

God damn, it had to be something like that, mused Rance. Aloud, he asked, 'Accident?'

For the first time some fire came into her eyes.

'He was murdered this morning. Shot down right in front of me!'

For the second time that night a chill swept through the marshal. Acts of

20

premeditated violence were rare in those parts but not unknown. Turning slightly to accept a cup of coffee, he happened to glance into the cell. No name's eyes were locked on to Angie's face with a feverish intensity. Was it the lust of a man for a comely young woman, or something else?

'His poor broken body is out there in the snow near our cabin,' she continued. 'I want you to find the bastard who did it and hang him. I want to see him twist and squeal at the end of a rope. I want it done *now*.'

An edge of hysteria had entered her voice which made it no easier for him to formulate a reply.

'I'm the *town* marshal, ma'am. I don't have any jurisdiction beyond its surveyed boundaries. Out there I'm just another private citizen.'

Shock registered on her face, but she had more to say.

'Then come with me as a man. The least we can do is bury him.'

'Not in this weather,' he replied

21

dubiously. 'The ground is rock hard.'

'Then help me lift him on to my wagon,' she persisted doggedly. 'He is . . . was a big man. I can't do it alone.'

He could resist no longer. It was his clear duty to help her and he knew it. A gentle smile creased his strong features. Whatever her problems, she was still damned attractive.

'Very well, I'll come. But not until morning when we can at least see.'

Something in his voice warned her not to argue, so she mutely nodded her acceptance. She well knew that his offer was the best that she was going to get from anybody decent on such a night. With the atmosphere notably strained and little else left to discuss, Rance offered to escort her to a rooming house, before going on to his own accommodation at the hotel.

Prior to leaving the jailhouse, he collected his shotgun and then carefully scrutinized the two men in the cell. Frock coat wordlessly returned his glance, before swinging on to a cot and closing his eyes. His partner remained apparently unconscious. Clem settled his ageing frame into the comfortable swivel chair with a sigh that suggested he would not be stirring again for some time. As Rance regarded his deputy, a vague unease settled over him.

'Don't you go letting those two loose, you hear? Not for anything. They stay right there until I get back!'

'They aren't going anywhere, Rance. You worry too much. I can handle them and any other drunk fellow who shows his face.'

3

As the new day dawned, the town of Devil's Lake found itself enveloped in a bitter stillness that seemed only to emphasize its isolation. The weekly stagecoach from Grand Forks, which was the only regular contact with the outside world, was long overdue. Silas Breckinridge, the grizzled livery operator, blamed road agents. Marshal Toller had his own theory. Leading his saddle horse through the double doors he commented, 'More than likely it's heavy snow, Silas. Besides, unless they hold up the stage within city limits I've no jurisdiction.'

How many times had he used that tired excuse to rid himself of unpleasant problems? As a forty-year-old veteran of some of the toughest cow towns, Rance had found a quiet corner to while away his middle age. No one bought or flouted the law in his town, but what happened beyond its limits was none of his concern. Yet here he was, on what was surely the coldest day of the winter so far, heading out into open country in the role of undertaker. Could it have had anything to do with the fact that he was accompanying an attractive newly widowed young woman?

Such thoughts would undoubtedly have persisted as he mounted up and trailed her wagon out of town had it not been for the bone-numbing chill. As it was, all he could think of was the stove in the jailhouse.

★   ★   ★

Angie's cabin, for it was now hers alone, stood a good hour's ride to the north, in a valley leading down to the lake from which the town drew both its name and its water. In milder weather it would have been undoubtedly pleasant. Jacob Sutter had picked his spot well. To Rance's jaundiced

25

eyes however, it now appeared dark and forbidding. An air of death hung over the place that wasn't entirely due to the frozen corpse sprawled in front of the doorway. Angie wheeled the flat bed farm wagon around next to her husband, but then seemed to freeze on the bench seat, overwhelming emotions obviously working within her. Awkwardly, Rance dismounted and made a cursory examination of the body.

'Have you moved him since . . . since it happened?'

A brief shake of the head was all she could manage as tears welled up in her eyes, but that was sufficient to indicate the direction he should take. Never comfortable with overt displays of emotion however justified, Rance remounted and gratefully urged his horse away from the homestead.

'I'll take a look around,' he called over his shoulder to the grieving widow.

★ ★ ★

He found what he was looking for some 400 yards away. In a large and conveniently secluded hollow, the snow had been flattened, as though a man had stretched out full length on it. Nearby, there were relatively fresh hoofprints. The lawman had hoped, but not really expected, to find a cartridge case. It was not to be. The assassin was obviously careful and probably made his own reloads. From the size of the entry wound, he had most likely used a Truthful Sharps rifle. However you viewed it, it was good shooting.

Then there was the mystery of the nighttime knock without any sign of footprints. Its intention was obvious: to draw someone out who might otherwise have lingered indoors at that time of year. Angie's only conversation on the way out had concerned her husband's horror at the lack of tracks around the cabin. Strange indentations in the snow leading back to the cabin provided an answer. Snowshoes. The killer was clever and had come prepared. What he couldn't do was completely hide the signs of his presence. There were two sets of tracks beyond the site of his dark deed. A laden horse had come in from the west and then headed back out again to the east. Following the outward tracks for a short distance soon convinced Rance that they would undoubtedly lead towards the town of Devil's Lake.

* * *

'Who else lives out here?'

Rance was setting a spell in the freezing cabin to get his breath back. Jacob Sutter had proved to be a great hulking bear of a man. The effort involved in heaving him on to the wagon had been considerable, even for a man of the marshal's powerful stature.

'A man named Chet Barclay has a small spread off to the east around the lake a ways,' replied Angie. 'Lives alone. I only met him the once and wouldn't care to again.'

Rance didn't ask why. He was too busy making uneasy assumptions. When he did respond, he had made up his mind.

'We'll look in on him before we head back to town. Best that we take your wagon along.'

Angie's only response was a penetrating gaze that spoke volumes.

★ ★ ★

They found the broken body of Chet Barclay near the entrance to his barn. The snow around his torso was stained with the blood from his horrific wounds.

'God damn, but those Sharps make a mess.'

Rance didn't normally approve of blasphemy, but these were not normal times. Two apparently unrelated men had been slain by the same weapon within a twenty-four hour period. Such things hadn't happened in Dakota since the Indian troubles.

Angie sat on the wagon seat, her face ashen. She had moved out West expecting hardship, but this was something else entirely. The fact that the dead man's valuable horses were whinnying for food in the large structure proved that the motive behind Barclay's murder was not just simple robbery. The marshal recalled the tracks heading back to his town and a sense of foreboding crept over him again. Such thoughts were getting to be an unpleasant habit.

'Pull the wagon around. We'll load this fellow on and take the horses too. Whatever they fetch at the livery will easily cover his funeral.'

'You think these killings are connected, don't you?'

He hadn't told her of his earlier findings, but she was obviously a smart lady and lying served no purpose.

'Yeah, I do. And what's more, I think the man that did them is in my town. Maybe even in my jail. What I don't know is why.'

As he recalled his easygoing deputy settling down for the night, a chill crept over him that had no connection to the weather. His inclination was to spur his mount back to Devil's Lake immediately. Yet in all conscience he could not leave Angie Sutter all alone with two dead men, one of whom was, unfortunately, her husband.

Swiftly dragging Barclay over to the wagon, he heaved the body on board. Dropping back to the ground, he ran back to his horse. His sudden sense of urgency did not go unnoticed.

'You fear for your deputy, don't you?'

Nodding tautly Rance replied, 'He's capable of locking up drunks and tending the jail, but he hasn't tasted real violence.'

'And you have?'

'Some,' he allowed.

Her eyes settled on his as she favoured him with a sad smile. 'And it's my fault that you're out here and not in town with him.'

He shook his head emphatically. 'No.

Whoever triggered the Sharps takes the blame for that, but you're going to have to work those horses some to stay with me.'

Her response to that was an emphatic nod that briefly warmed his heart. Then they were off through the snow and that dreadful anxiety returned.

4

The weak sun had already past its apogee by the time they returned to the remote town. At that latitude its power did little to assuage the dead hand of winter, but Rance was oblivious to the vicious chill. Although officially a marshal again, he now actually dreaded what he might find. As Angie's wagon with its gruesome cargo rattled through the slush on Main Street, he slid from the saddle and took a deep breath. Professional instinct urged him to slow down, so he cast a watchful eye over the surrounding wooden buildings. Despite the hour, not a single person was in view, which was very odd. Even in such harsh conditions the business of life went on. A sixth sense nagged him to tether his mount out of sight behind the jail. This accomplished, he returned to the jailhouse entrance. Still he didn't go inside. Quietly, he instructed Angie to wheel her rig around so that it was facing back out of town. If asked, he couldn't have explained why. It just seemed to make sense. Only then was he ready. His heart was pounding violently. Barging open the heavy door, Rance stepped into his office.

The interior appeared *almost* as he had left it. Clem sat dozing in the swivel chair. The stove held a cheery glow and the gun rack was locked just as it should be. Relief surged through him. Yet as his eyes adjusted to the gloom everything began to unravel. The cell to the rear no longer had any occupants. Clem's jacket appeared to be coated in a dark substance. Unable to speak, Rance slowly tilted the chair back. His deputy shifted position. As his head lolled back the huge gaping slit in his throat was displayed for all to see.

Choking back a cry of horror, Rance tore his glance away and strode to the cell. The heavy key was in the lock. Dark stains were visible on the board floor. The town's only remaining lawman seized the iron bars in a vicious grip. His mind was a seething maelstrom, but out of it came some logical thought. It was highly unlikely that the two prisoners had been able to talk their way out. Clem might have been lazy, but he wasn't a complete idiot. Which meant that they had help, and whoever it was could well be still in town along with the escaped prisoners. Opposition numbers were increasing and he no longer had any back up. The implications of all that turned in his belly like a screw.

From behind him there came a gasp of shock. Twisting round like a cat he beheld Angie Sutter staring wide-eyed at yet another bloody corpse. Rushing forward, his intention was to usher her out of the office. What stopped him was the sudden realization that for the moment there was nowhere else for her to go.

'Ma'am, do you know how to use that Henry?'

'As well as any other woman who chooses to live in the wilds,' she answered defiantly. 'And my name is Angie.'

A fleeting smile touched his face. She would do.

'Very well, *Angie*. From now on we stay together at all times. I believe that the man who killed your husband also killed Clem, or at least was a party to it. I actually had him locked up and I went for a ride, God damn it.'

'You could not possibly have known,' she replied with a certainty that impressed him.

'Maybe not,' he allowed. 'But from now on we don't take any chances.'

With that he strode to the window and carefully perused the street. Still not a soul about. His town seemed to be in the grip of a strange malaise. Then an idea seized him. No horses were left outdoors in such weather; therefore the livery owner would be doing good business and would also know all the comings and goings.

'We're heading for the stables,' he

stated. 'Follow me, but stay a few yards back. We'll be less of a target that way.'

'What about your deputy? We can't just leave him like that.'

'My only aim right now is keeping you and me alive,' he replied forcefully. Then in a softer tone he added, 'So he stays where he lays.'

* * *

Like a man and his shadow they swept along the boardwalk. His eyes roamed everywhere. Past the barber's, the milliner's store and then the bank. He was aware of people in those buildings, which was something. It meant that the whole town had not just up and left. But unusually everyone kept their eyes averted, as though he was suddenly a pariah. Under normal circumstances he would have been in there probing, asking questions, but something told him to maintain his course.

On the point of entering the livery, he

abruptly stopped in his tracks. Directly across the street was the telegraph office. A visit there could definitely not go amiss. As he crossed the open space, his eyes instinctively scanned the surrounding buildings. For the first time since taking up his employment in Devil's Lake, he felt a real sense of danger.

Jonas Hardacre's eyes almost popped out of their sockets as he reluctantly greeted the town marshal. A wizened individual with bad teeth, he wore bottle-bottomed wire-rimmed spectacles that greatly accentuated his watery orbs. They shone even more when Angie crowded into the small office. Remembering his manners, the telegraph operator tapped a forefinger to his temple. Marshal Toller's keen glance took in the clear desk, the inert telegraph key and the silent relay system. Normally, Jonas existed in a veritable blizzard of paper. Normally.

'Taking a holiday, Jonas?' Rance enquired drily.

Jonas's sparsely covered skull bobbed up and down nervously as he cleared his throat to respond. 'Might just as well, Marshal. The line's been down two days now. Must be the snow.'

'The same snow that's delayed the stage, maybe. Tell me,' asked the lawman conversationally, 'how long's it likely to stay down?'

Jonas's forehead wrinkled under the effort of a considered reply. 'That all depends on how long it takes for the linesmen to find the break.'

Turning for the door, Rance remarked, 'Who knows, they just might find the Grand Forks stage while they're out there.'

* * *

Silas Breckinridge's eyes bulged as the lawman entered his premises. He desperately tried to raise a smile, yet singularly failed in the attempt. His narrow whiskery face habitually wore a pessimistic expression, which was definitely in the ascendant that day.

Threadbare clothes covered his spare frame. It was hard to credit that as sole owner of the livery he was one of the wealthiest men in town. His jaw began to work on a greeting, but then Angie Sutter arrived and he gave up the attempt. Instead he gazed at her curiously, as though struggling to understand the reason for her presence.

Rance regarded him carefully as he spoke. 'Lost your tongue, Silas? You usually have some words of wisdom for the weary traveller.'

The sarcasm was plainly evident and quite deliberate. He was trying to provoke an unguarded response. When none was forthcoming he tried again.

'Any new mounts in here recently? Come on Silas, you don't miss anything that goes on in this town.'

'Some,' allowed the other in a croaky voice. 'I'm not here all the time though. I know one thing . . . the stage still hasn't arrived. It's never been this overdue.'

Rance contemplated him thoughtfully. Was Silas trying to convey something other than just his concern for the missing stagecoach? The livery operator was plainly scared, but not of the marshal. He tried a different tack.

'There's a string of horses outside the jail. They belong to a certain Chet Barclay whose spread is to the north of here. You might care to look them over and make an offer, but *don't* go inside. I'll come find you later.'

Something in that discourse touched a nerve. Silas's face had literally turned grey. The question was how many murders did he know about. One thing was for sure: he'd get the shock of his life if he peered into Angie's wagon.

Glancing at her, Rance stated, 'It's time we visited Pearsall's. Any dark deeds around here generally involve that place. Are you up to it?'

'Don't you worry about me, Marshal Toller,' she replied firmly. 'This thing needs seeing through.'

God, she's got spunk, he marvelled.

Husband slaughtered before her eyes and already she's my new deputy!

As the two of them turned away Silas called out hesitantly, 'Be careful, Marshal.'

★　★　★

Pushing open the heavy livery door, Rance stepped out on to the deserted street. Watching intently for any sign of life, he misjudged his footing in the slush. He right leg slid sideways and the ground rushed up to him. The sudden blast of pressure by his left ear only added to his confusion. The projectile that had caused it slammed into the door behind him. From way off across the street came the sound of a heavy detonation. The lawman was under fire . . . from a Sharps rifle!

'You're a dead man, Toller!'

Realization struck him as to just who that was. He also knew that he had to decide whether to advance or retreat. From other buildings across the frozen thoroughfare rifle shots blasted out. Bullets peppered the ground around him, forcing his decision. Rushing a single shot buffalo gun was one thing, repeating rifles entirely another. Twisting round like an eel, Rance half crawled back into the building. Angie looked on in surprise, but there was no sign of panic on her face. Getting gingerly to his feet, Rance tested his leg. It would answer.

'I need you to stand guard,' he said, watching her carefully. 'If you get the chance of a shot take it, but don't waste cartridges.' Then in a louder voice, 'I need to have words with Silas.'

That man nervously retreated across the stables. Horses were whinnying with fright, but they might as well not have existed. His face twisted with fear, the proprietor had eyes only for Rance. The marshal backed his prey up to a massive wooden beam. Placing the muzzles of his shotgun under the man's chin he rasped out a question.

'How many are out there?'

Silas appeared on the point of collapse but just managed a response.

'Maybe a dozen, maybe more. They call themselves regulators.'

'Why?' The question was only one word, but it had massive significance. Any positive response was likely to provide answers to the murders out by the lake. As if to add emphasis, Angie's rifle barked out in defiance. Increasing the pressure on his weapon, Rance's eyes bored into those of the other man. 'It would behove you to answer me!'

'Gold!' The frightened man shouted the word, as though anxious to rid himself of it. 'There's a gold strike just to the north. They want the town but not the law. Just like it was in Deadwood.'

With the mention of that particular settlement suddenly it all fell into place. Deadwood had burst into vigorous life without any official sanction some years before down in Indian Territory. Certain people had grown rich, completely unfettered by any laws or statutes. If colour had been discovered near Devil's Lake they would doubtless want to replicate their success. So apparently they had sent in their so-called regulators to gain control.

Bullets smashed into the exterior of the structure, but Angie gamely stood her ground by the door and loosed off another shot. Silas, having once started talking now could not stop.

'We told them that we would co-operate. This place could become a boom town. There's money to be made for God's sake, but then they heard that you were a hard ass. That you wouldn't bend and couldn't be bought. Locking up the regulators' leader only proved it to them.'

Everything was now so clear.

'And they killed Barclay and Sutter to get their land for free,' stated Rance bitterly.

'K-k-killed them?' stuttered Silas. 'They were supposed to buy them out. Oh my God, this is terrible.'

'How do you think she feels?' Rance

gestured towards Angie. 'That's Sutter's widow.'

Silas looked physically sick. The harsh brutal reality of unfettered big business hit home.

There was another burst of gunfire outside and Rance knew that they needed to be off. He just had one more question.

'Who's the leader of that gang of bar trash?'

The skin tightened around Silas's scrawny neck as he grimaced.

'Dan Bodeen. A killer for hire by all accounts. You ever heard of him?'

Rance had heard of him all right. He'd also had him locked up in his jail. Cursing under his breath, he made up his mind. Up against an unknown number of professional gunmen, they only really had one option.

'Lead the *regulators*' horses over to the entrance.'

The livery operator appeared completely nonplussed.

'Do it,' barked the lawman, prodding

46

upwards with his shotgun, 'or you won't see another day!'

As the shaken individual began to comply, Rance ran over to Angie, who was diligently watching the street. Touching her lightly on the shoulder he remarked, 'We're going to need more ammunition before we leave town. When these horses take off, we run for the jailhouse.'

Her pale eyes briefly met his. He was asking too much of her and he knew it. Yet what other option did he have? Somehow a group of desperados had taken over his town without him even realizing it. If she tried to return to her cabin as things stood, she would likely only end up in a cold hole in the ground along with her husband.

By chivvying Silas along, they finally ended up with a dozen or so nervous, restless horses milling around the double doors. Getting behind them, Rance raised his shotgun and discharged one barrel. Such a tremendous indoor blast left his ears ringing with pain, but did achieve the desired result. The startled animals surged forward away from the frightening detonation. As their assailants' horses galloped out on to the main street, Rance and Angie slipped off to the left heading for the boardwalk and ultimately the jail.

Gunshots rang out across the thoroughfare, but none of the projectiles came anywhere near them. The confused stampede had destroyed any chance of accurate fire. As the two fugitives breathlessly reached their destination, Rance triggered the second barrel of his shotgun for effect. His aim was vague, but it kept heads down as they piled in through the door. Slamming it shut he took a quick glance around. Everything appeared as it had been, including the gruesome occupant of the swivel chair.

'Drop the big gun, law dog. You, bitch, shuck the rifle!'

The gravelly voice came from within the cell and sent shock waves through both of them. In the unlit gloom Rance was tempted to make a move, but recognized both the futility of it and the danger to Angie. The intervening bars were no defence against powder and ball, and unlike the marshal their captor's eyes were adjusted to the indifferent light. Reluctantly he let his weapon slip to the floor and she followed suit. Rance had no particular concerns about relinquishing his shotgun, as it was empty. His Remington was another matter.

'Now the belt. Unbuckle and let it slide.'

In conjunction with those words a heavy set individual materialized from the back of the cell. Rance received another shock of recognition. It was the previous night's drunkard back on his feet. His naturally unpleasant features, heavily brutalized by life, did not fill his two prisoners with confidence.

'Yeah, it's me,' he drawled. 'That was one hell of a sock-doggler you gave me, Marshal. My head's been aching fit to burst all morning. I'd just as soon shoot

49

you now, but Bodeen wants a parley first. He ain't going to get one though, unless you put some distance between you and that handgun.'

As though emphasizing his deadly intent, he took a straight-arm aim at the lawman's head.

He'll do it too, decided Rance grimly. Slowly he released his gunbelt. Letting it drop gently to the floor, he kicked it over towards the cell.

The burly gun thug favoured him with a cold smile.

'I guess you weren't quite ready to be paroled to Jesus,' he sneered. 'Now go stand over there next to your deputy, whilst I take a closer look at this little gal.'

With a great show of reluctance, Rance edged over towards Clem's body. Satisfied, his captor moved in on Angie. Although obviously frightened she stood her ground.

'I reckon I'm just going to have to search you for hidden weapons, lady. Undo that buffalo robe!'

Her eyes widened in horror and she looked desperately over at Rance's apparently impotent form.

'Look at me, not him,' snarled her tormentor. Despite the cold, a sheen of sweat had appeared on his top lip. His beady eyes studied her intently as he pulled back the heavy coat. It was quite obvious what he was really searching for.

With a leer he placed his hand on her thigh. 'I'm going to enjoy this!'

'Tatum, are they under your gun or what?'

At the sound of that familiar voice, the man that they now knew as Tatum froze. Then, furtively, he turned towards the window, a look of alarm spreading across his bovine features. Rance stared pointedly at Angie. As their eyes met he rolled his to the right, indicating that she should move away from her oppressor. As she complied, two things happened: Tatum glanced rapidly her way and Rance drew Clem's revolver and shot the man squarely in his chest.

In such an enclosed space, the roaring discharge was acutely painful. Through the plume of sulphurous smoke, Rance observed Tatum on the floor, his body twitching in its death throes. Swiftly picking up the fallen man's revolver, he handed it to Angie.

'You might find that useful,' he remarked laconically.

Her horrified gaze was fixed on the dying man, yet instinctively she accepted the weapon.

Rance nodded approvingly before glancing over at Clem's rigid corpse. Thankfully, no one had thought to disarm a dead man. So, even though devoid of all life, his deputy had still managed to come to their aid. Yet sadly there was no time for sentimental reflection. Confused shouting came from the street. He had mere seconds to react.

Grabbing his shotgun, Rance broke it and replaced the two cartridges. Retracting both hammers, he tucked the butt tightly into his shoulder. On his command, Angie threw open the jailhouse door. Four men with drawn weapons were advancing cautiously towards him. The powerful figure of Dan Bodeen, in his black frock coat, was furthest away. Sheer horror registered on the faces of his men, as they comprehended the deadly threat. Without the slightest hesitation Rance squeezed both triggers.

Even through the tremendous discharge, he noticed Bodeen deftly move behind his nearest accomplice. The twin blast caught the three at the front. Two died instantly, their features reduced to a bloody pulp, whilst the third took some shot in his left shoulder. He would be out of it, but not for long unless gangrene took hold. Ignoring his wounded compatriot, Bodeen ran for cover, blood trickling from his right ear.

His shoulder aching from the brutal recoil, Rance slammed the door shut and swiftly reloaded the twelve gauge. Angie stood before him, anxiety etched on her pale features. Recognizing her need for encouragement, he favoured her with a warm smile. Patting the stock of his weapon, he remarked, 'Ain't this a real crowd-pleaser?'

She just managed a strained grimace. Still in shock from her husband's death, the sudden outbreak of bloody violence was too much to absorb.

'What now?' Her question was subdued.

Without faltering he replied, 'We take everything we need and go. Now, while they're hurting.'

'Go? Go where?' Angie appeared dazed and he knew that for both their sakes he had to snap her out of it.

'We can't stay here. They can blast us out, burn us out, or even starve us out. Any way you look at it we'd be finished. There's too many of them and we don't even know where they are. We need to draw them out after us. Spread them out and tear them up some.'

Her eyes widened as she took in his little speech.

'We can't survive the night out of doors,' he continued remorselessly, 'so we'll head for your cabin. And that's enough talk. We're leaving *now*!'

So saying, he removed a Winchester .44-.40 carbine from the gun rack and began emptying the drawers of ammunition. As though awakened from a trance, Angie stuffed some of it in her pockets and recovered her Henry.

'Run for the wagon and hightail it,' instructed Rance. 'I'll cover you, then follow.'

Flinging the door open, he raised his shotgun. Angie dashed out and clambered on to the rig. No gunfire greeted them. The so-called regulators had taken casualties and were spread out across the town. The sudden move appeared to have taken them by surprise.

Angie got the team rolling and headed north out of town. With a weapon in each hand, Rance pounded down the boardwalk. As he reached the corner, the first shot rang out. It sounded very much like a Sharps. The heavy bullet slammed into the timber next to his head.

'You've made me bleed. You're a dead man, Toller!'

Bodeen's deep voice followed him round the back of the jailhouse. Sheathing the Winchester, Rance mounted up and spurred his horse. The beast stumbled slightly, found its footing in the snow and then picked up speed. As they broke cover from behind the building, Rance fired one barrel from his shotgun for effect and then kept his head down. A ragged fusillade rattled out, but none of the projectiles came close. Knowing full well the effective range of a Sharps Rifle, he held the gallop until he was well clear.

Up ahead he could make out the wagon careening across the desolate landscape. Angie appeared to handle a team with great competence. She could also shoot and didn't talk too much. All those accomplishments were useful assets, which remarkably enough, had assisted both of them in escaping from the settlement unscathed. However, it couldn't be denied that their prospects still looked decidedly bleak. They were up against numerous hired guns in the pay of ruthless big business. His only deputy was dead and the townspeople appeared to have sold out on the quiet. Devil's Lake was no longer the soft option that he had supposed. In fact there seemed to be only one redeeming feature on the horizon: *she* happened to be called Angie, and was at that very moment expecting him at her side.

5

As Marshal Rance Toller gazed down on the two frozen cadavers in the wagon bed, he wondered just when they might secure a final resting place. The thought of Angie continually transporting her dead husband was just too macabre. Jacob Sutter really should have got himself shot in summer when grave digging was actually possible. It also occurred to him that he was now a marshal without a town. The good citizens of Devil's Lake could no longer be relied upon to back his play. Yet just riding off into the sunset was not an option. Such a man as Dan Bodeen was unlikely to leave him alone after all that had transpired and he would also have recognized his mistake in leaving Angie alive. It was never a wise move to murder a woman, but the speculators needed her property. And then there was Clem. Whatever happened to the town, Rance could not in all conscience allow his senseless killing to go unpunished. Brutal bloody violence had once been a way of life that he had thought was consigned to the past. Unfortunately those days had returned, and all because someone had discovered that damned yellow metal. Gold had an unpleasant habit of turning men into devils. Those now controlling the find had done a remarkable job of keeping it quiet. Isolation and weather had undoubtedly helped them, but mostly it would have been intimidation.

The desolate snow-covered hills held a raw beauty, but also provided Rance with opportunity. Calling on Angie to slow down, he pulled alongside. Her careworn features were still remarkably attractive, but now was not the time for such thoughts.

'I'm going to tie my horse to your wagon and hitch a ride. When I see the right spot I'll drop off and wait on events.'

Her eyes widened in alarm, a reaction that was getting to be a habit. 'You think they might be following us?'

Dropping on to the bench seat next to her he replied, 'Oh, they're on our trail all right. I might be able to catch them in an ambuscade, though that'll depend on who's leading them, I guess.'

For a few moments neither of them spoke. Rance was scrutinizing the land whilst Angie had her hands full with the team. Then he saw it.

'You see up ahead where the ground slopes away? I'll drop off there. You keep on going until you're out of sight. Then rein in and wait for me. If they get past me it means that I'm dead and you're on your own.'

That had come out far more brutally than he had intended and suddenly she looked so very vulnerable. Favouring him with a sad smile she replied, 'I understand.'

Gripping both Winchester and shot-gun, he rasped out, 'Pull up!'

As he jumped off the board and into

the deep snow Angie called out, 'Good luck.'

* * *

There is only so long a man can lie still in snow before he became like the fellows on Angie's wagon. The intense cold was eating into his bones. Both hammers were cocked on his scatter-gun, but it was a toss up which would freeze first: those or his fingers. Yet he could not under any circumstances start to move about. Bodeen could be scanning the terrain with a spyglass at that very moment. Rance had to keep his mind off the bitter conditions and on something else. An image of Angie's face came into his head. 'God, but she's a fine-looking woman. Yet how can I be thinking about her with her husband still above ground?' Guilt crowded into his mind, but at least it kept him occupied.

Time passed and he began to think that he was freezing to death for nothing. He was seriously thinking of giving up and trudging back to the wagon, when movement suddenly registered on his peripheral vision. Without turning his head, he glanced sideways. And there they were. Six horsemen taking their own sweet time. Bodeen had a man on point, whilst he carefully perused the tracks before him. The other four were spread out, thereby minimizing themselves as a target. Rance decided that he would have to settle for one, or maybe two at most. Carefully shifting his gun, he lined up on the nearest regulator.

Bodeen reined in and leaned sideways out of the saddle. Something specific had caught his attention. Returning upright, he savagely spurred his horse and bellowed out, 'We're made! Get the hell out of it.'

All six men swung away and galloped hell for leather towards town.

'Damn, damn, damn,' intoned Rance, as he discarded the shotgun. Grabbing the Winchester, he sighted down on to the nearest of the fleeing men. Then, as the distance widened, he lowered the barrel slightly to cover the much larger animal and squeezed off a shot. The weapon's roar shattered the frozen stillness around him. The horse slewed sideways, throwing its rider to the ground. Levering another cartridge into the breach, Rance waited for the disorientated gunman to stagger to his feet. Backlit by the virgin snow, the man presented a perfect target. Firing again, Rance did not need to see through the plume of smoke to know that he had struck his prey. He had never missed a shot like that.

For the first time, he regretted not owning the rifle version of his 1873 Winchester. The twenty-inch carbine was far more convenient for town use, but right then he could have used an extra four inches of barrel length. As it was, the others were out of range so it was time to go. He grabbed his shotgun and rose up stiffly from the snow. Forcing himself into vigorous movement, Rance took off towards Angie.

The Sharps! Even as the thought struck him like an anvil, he threw himself to the ground. He felt the blast of concussion as the heavy bullet passed over. Three times he had narrowly escaped death from that bloody gun. He could not gamble on being given a fourth.

Counting out the Sharps reloading time, he leapt to his feet and ran like hell. If seven league boots had existed outside of fairy-tales he would have given any amount for a pair. To his left he saw a depression in the ground. Dropping into it, he found himself waist high in crisp snow. He ducked down in anticipation of the next shot, but, of course, it didn't come. Bodeen was too much of a professional to waste ammunition on wild shooting.

A voice in the distance boomed out with the now familiar taunt: 'You're a dead man, Toller!'

With that derisive cry eating into him and his face covered in snow, Rance felt an incandescent rage welling up inside of him. It was the sort of rage that could easily bring about his death, and was best channelled instead into getting him out of there. Shaking his head, he kept low and ploughed off through the deep snow. The light was beginning to drain out of the winter sky, which meant that the five remaining horsemen were unlikely to continue their pursuit. The spread pattern of his double-barrelled shotgun was far more dangerous in the dark than the precision shooting afforded by a Sharps rifle.

The deep gully finally levelled out, making the going easier. By that time he felt confident that Bodeen would be unable to draw a bead on him. Then, to his great relief, he spotted the wagon waiting in the distance. Despite the conditions, he broke into a trot. As he drew closer Rance could make out Angie anxiously watching him. Somehow he felt that she was as glad to see him, as he was to see her.

'I heard shooting,' she remarked,

concern etched on her face.

'That's usual in an ambush,' he replied, and then immediately regretted it. He was still angry from his third brush with death. She was shivering from the cold and maybe something else. And now her concern had been replaced by hurt.

'Damn it!'

He wanted to put his arms around her, but knew that that was unacceptable. Instead he tried again. 'I'm sorry. That Bodeen's some *hombre*. Nearly caught me again with that buffalo gun. He must have seen something in the tracks. He knew I'd dropped back.'

'Well he didn't get you and you're here now,' she responded, her eyes locked on his.

'I am, and he's lost one more dead. Which means that the only thing we have to fear tonight is the cold. We need to get to your cabin.'

So saying, he sheathed his Winchester and mounted up. The shotgun remained across the saddle horn as always. When hunting outlaws or Indians, you could never tell when they might choose to rush you and the habit had stayed with him.

Angie got the team moving. In such conditions they all, humans and animals, needed food and shelter and thankfully it was not far away.

6

Darkness had fallen by the time they came within sight of the cabin. A hazy moon cast an eerie glow over the frozen lake. In such conditions it was easy to understand why the dirt worshippers believed that the vast expanse of water contained monsters and evil spirits. A form of malevolence had certainly visited the owners of the homestead.

Although Rance and Angie had reached their destination, their mutual relief was to be short-lived. It took a considerable amount of concentration to control the wagon team on such a night, so consequently it was the lawman who made the discovery.

'Did you leave a lamp burning this morning?'

Angie abruptly reined in the team, causing them to stamp about skittishly.

'You know I didn't,' she replied

resolutely. 'You were there. We just kept the door open.'

As they sat staring in the relative silence, two more things became apparent: smoke curled up out of the chimney, and the sound of raucous laughter drifted towards them. Angie gasped in alarm and reached for her rifle.

'Those devils mean to kill me and take what is ours!'

Unconsciously her glance flitted back towards her husband's body. Rance, who was endeavouring to ignore that particular cadaver's continued presence, had his own theory.

'If Bodeen's men were lying in wait, your home would be in darkness. No, this is something else. Those pus weasels aren't expecting trouble; they're having a celebration.'

'So what are we to do?' she demanded. There was an edge to her voice that suggested she already had ideas on that score.

Rance hunched forward in his saddle

and sighed. It had been a long and arduous day. Bloody violence had made an unwelcome return to his life. He needed a warm stove and some hot food. Yet now it appeared that he might have to fight for both commodities. Damn it all to hell! he blasphemed silently.

And yet there was an alternative. Glancing down at Angie he remarked, 'We know for a fact that the Barclay spread is empty.'

He nearly added that they had that particular landowner with them, but thought better of it.

'How about we spend the night there and then face this trouble in the morning? With luck they'll be hung over and we can just walk on in.'

Angie glared up at him. Even in the gloom, her eyes seemed to flash with anger. 'What kind of marshal are you? That's my home. I want those men out now, and if you won't do it, I will!'

So saying, she worked the lever

action of the Henry and clambered off the bench seat.

Rance sighed long and hard. She really was a ball breaker. Recognizing her serious intent, he rapidly dismounted and grabbed her arm. When he spoke, there was a hard edge to his words.

'You've got a real harsh tongue, lady. I know you've had it tough, but don't take it out on me. Right now I'm all you've got!'

She made to interrupt him, but he tightened his grip and ploughed on.

'You don't know who or how many are in that cabin. If you bust in there in a conniption fit, you'll like as not end up in the back of that wagon with your husband.'

Her anger dissolved to be replaced by anguish. Inner turmoil worked on her as she turned away. Releasing his grip, he allowed her to drift over to the rear of the wagon. From the cabin there came a pretty impressive rebel yell. Its new occupants didn't sound much of a threat to anyone, but then such things were notoriously hard to predict. Someone 'liquored up' could turn in a hair's breadth. His mind made up, Rance rejoined Angie. She was staring intently at the largest of the shiny frozen bodies. It occurred to Rance that they would be best off in the lake along with any casualties from the imminent repossession.

'We'll get your cabin back,' he stated softly. 'But we'll do it my way, savvy?'

Her eyes widened in surprise. The fresh tears on her cheeks glinted in the moonlight. And then it all came out. 'You shouldn't ought to talk to me like you did. Two days ago I was still married to that man. We were going to have a family. They had no call to do what they did. They could have mined the gold. We wouldn't have stopped them.'

A racking sob interrupted her flow. If Jacob Sutter had been any kind of man he would have wanted his share all right, considered Rance but he held his tongue. Tearing her eyes away from the wagon, Angie drew in a deep breath and seemed to gain control of herself.

'Very well, *Marshal*. We'll do it your way.'

He scrutinized her carefully. If they were going to proceed then it had to be done properly.

'Fair enough. This is how it's going to be. Wait until I get out of sight round the side of the cabin. Then you trundle on in as though you're returning from town. No weapons mind. You do some hollering, like you're surprised to find them there. They come out and I get the drop on them. Easy!'

Even as he was speaking a voice in the recesses of his mind was telling him that when liquor and guns mix nothing is easy.

Leaving his horse tethered to the wagon, Rance removed the glove from his right hand. Taking the shotgun in a two-handed grip, he slowly made his way towards the cabin. To him, every step taken in the crisp snow sounded deafening. He needn't have worried. Even with the solid door closed the shouting and cussing were clearly audible.

Angie placed her rifle in the back of the wagon next to Jacob. The revolver that Rance had given her nestled in the small of her back. She had no intention of confronting some desperadoes unarmed. Watching the marshal as he carefully made his way round the front of her cabin, she began to regret having instigated their course of action. The possibility of more violence prompted a hotchpotch of thoughts to race through her mind. Hadn't enough men died in the last few days? Rance Toller was undoubtedly a brave and capable man, but he was now risking his life solely on her behalf. The horrific demise of his deputy might have been avoided if she had not persuaded Rance to leave town with her. Then again she had noticed the way he looked at her. He may well have had an ulterior motive for helping her, but with Jacob still unburied such thoughts were entirely premature. Still, it couldn't be denied that the west was no place for a woman alone.

He was out of sight, which meant that he must be in position. If she didn't make a move soon her courage would seep away. Gripping the reins, Angie urged the team forward. The wagon clattered along the rock-hard ground. There was no sign of any horses, which meant that unless the men had walked, they must have stabled them in her barn. The thought of that made her blood boil. The anger coursing through her fuelled a boldness out of all proportion to her offensive capabilities. Dragging the wagon to a halt directly in front of her door, Angie stood up and yelled out, 'Who's in my god-damned house? Show yourselves, or I'll tip coal tar down the chimney!'

Inside the house there was a brief stunned silence, followed by a very distinct response.

'Hot dang, we've got us a female outside!'

There was a stampede for the entrance and the door was flung open. Flickering light flooded the scene and three partially clad ruffians crowded out. Their bloodshot eyes were everywhere: on her, then the wagon, followed by the immediate area and then back on to her. Having finally settled on Angie, they appeared to be almost drinking her in.

The trio's apparent leader, a hairy beast of a man clad only in long-johns remarked, 'Look who's come to visit. We've got us our very own painted lady. Yee haa!'

The other two tried to push past him to get a better view.

'Don't push me, you sons of bitches,' he snarled at them. 'I saw her first.'

As his lustful eyes fixed on hers, he reached out a grubby hand.

'Come on, darling. I need a poke. Get yourself down off that wagon.'

Real fear lanced into her. The men obviously meant her harm and Rance was nowhere to be seen.

The leader of the men lurched forward. His tone changed abruptly.

'Don't you hear too good, bitch? Get down here now, or I'll drag you off and give you a slap for the trouble.'

At that point the situation became irretrievable. Cursing Rance's apparent absence, Angie reached behind her for Tatum's revolver. Dragging it clear of her bulky coat, she levelled the heavy piece at the beast and squeezed the trigger. When nothing whatsoever happened her fear seemed to increase tenfold. With a sneer the brute stepped nearer and took her right ankle in a vice-like grip.

'That's a Colt Army, bitch. You need to cock it first.'

From his condescendingly teasing manner, she instinctively knew that he didn't think she would do it. Desperately pulling the hammer back to full cock, Angie again squeezed the trigger. With a roar the weapon bucked in her hand. The soft lead ball took him just below the bridge of his nose, literally destroying his features, whilst the powder flash set his greasy hair smouldering. A warm substance splashed on her face and she screamed. One of the others called out, 'Sweet Jesus, she actually did it!'

From the side of the cabin, Rance aimed his shotgun. He had deliberately stayed his hand as he waited for all of them to come into view. The unexpected gunshot took him by surprise and also started a chain reaction. As the echoes of the discharge died away he heard a loud thump in the cabin. Then the window shutters just behind him exploded outwards as a burly figure smashed through them. Twisting around, Rance instinctively fired once. The spread of shot caught his assailant in the groin at point-blank range. With an agonized wail that man collapsed in the snow, no longer a threat to anyone.

The concussive blast had the two at the front peering into the darkness in horror, but there was more to come. Angie's blood was well and truly up.

Without sighting down on anyone in particular she repeatedly cocked and fired the revolver. Large calibre lead balls smacked into the snow, whilst the air was filled with powdersmoke. Desperate to avoid the fusillade, the two men were reduced to cowering on the ground. Only after she had dry fired on three empty chambers did she finally desist.

Rance found her slumped on the wagon seat in a state of mild shock. Reaching up, he eased the empty revolver from her unresisting fingers. Tossing it into the wagon bed, he then turned to cover her two victims with his shotgun. He needn't have troubled himself. Neither appeared to be hit; yet any fight that might have existed had left them both.

Despite the adrenalin-inducing violence, Rance had retained a clear head. Something about the turn of events was gnawing on him: why Angie's cabin and on that specific night?

If ever there was a fortuitous time to

question the two men it was now. Their leader's brain matter was coating the slush, whilst their companion lay curled up in a foetal position begging to die. Looming over them, Rance prodded them both hard in the ribs with his sawn-off.

'Better make your peace with God, boys, because I ain't taking any prisoners this night!'

Both men peered up at him. One of them, a scrawny individual with the look of a consumptive, began to blubber. The other possessed a little more grit and was at least able to form some words.

'You've got no call to kill us, mister. We've done you no harm.'

'What just happens to bring you here on this particular night?' Rance demanded sharply.

'We needed somewhere to fort up and he told us the place was empty.'

Rance's heart began to pound harder as he followed that up. '*Who* told you?'

'Bodeen. He said we could stay here

as long as we needed.'

From the side of the building an agonized voice cried out, 'For pity's sake kill me!'

Rance ignored him. He had more important matters on his mind.

'Why here? Why not in town? What are you hiding from?'

The other man viewed him appraisingly. His pock marked features displayed a certain native cunning. His reply suggested that he was getting over his immediate fear. 'What's all that to you? Are you some kind of law?'

'Kill me!' The plea came from a soul in torment.

Rance made up his mind. Addressing the newly emboldened thug, he remarked dryly, 'You and me are going to talk some more. Stay put!'

Smoothly drawing and cocking his Remington, Rance turned away and approached the horribly wounded individual. Even in the poor light there was no mistaking the vast quantity of blood that he had shed. Something in the marshal's firm resolve had registered with Angie. Still recumbent on the bench seat, she called out, 'Rance, what are you about?'

Ignoring her, he levelled his revolver. Even though out of his mind with pain and shock, his victim somehow sensed the movement and looked up. The tortured, twisted features no longer belonged to a human being. Rance's weapon crashed out once. The devastating headshot finished what the other man had started by his leaping through the window. Holstering his gun, the lawman grimly returned to his two prisoners.

'You're Rance Toller, the marshal from Devil's Lake.' It was a statement rather than a question. 'They say you're a hard nose.'

Nodding slowly, Rance replied, 'That I am. And if I have to draw this smoke wagon again, you two boys will both be mustered out.'

In the light of his recent action, his words suddenly carried considerable weight and they both remained silent.

'Now then, just what have you done for Dan Bodeen?'

Surprisingly it was the consumptive who replied. 'We held up the stage from Grand Forks.'

Ice water formed in Rance's veins as he responded. 'That stage wasn't just late; it never turned up.'

The two road agents glanced apprehensively at each other, but the one who had finally found his voice now just couldn't stop. 'It wasn't our fault,' he whined. 'The guard drew down on us with some kind of god-damned blunderbuss and then one of the passengers backed his play. Silly bastard must have valued his watch more than his life.'

'So they're all dead?' asked Rance curtly.

'It kind of worked out that way,' replied the other quietly, before giggling inanely.

Rance turned away in disgust and found himself face to face with Angie.

'I heard it all,' she said. 'These men are less than animals.'

That suddenly gave him an idea. 'So they can spend the night in the barn, tethered tight!'

That was greeted with a storm of protest. 'Sweet Jesus, Marshal. There's no heat in there. We'll freeze solid.'

Training his shotgun on them, Rance favoured them with a bleak smile. 'So don't rob and kill innocent people. Now move while you still can!'

*   *   *

The blissful heat from the iron stove enveloped him as he stepped into the cabin. Angie, the practical frontier wife, was stirring a pan of beans. Coffee was on the boil and the open shutters had been secured. The road agents had not been in possession long enough to foul her home. She glanced over at him and smiled.

Yeah, he thought. I was right the first time. She's as pretty as a peach.

Concern briefly clouded her features but not, as it turned out, for him.

'Those skunks might die out there in my barn on such a night.'

'Likely they could at that,' he allowed. 'But they aren't setting foot in here again. Anyhow, death would be fair reward for their bad deeds.'

'You're a hard man, Marshal Toller,' she remarked without any apparent resentment.

'I've had a hard life,' he replied. 'Besides, you wanted them evicted. I was all for moving on. Oh, and I prefer Rance to Marshal Toller.'

'And what you want you usually get, I should think,' she responded swiftly, gesturing for him to be seated at the solid wooden table.

Scooping up beans with a chunk of bread, he finished the exchange with, 'If I did I wouldn't be marshalling in a one-horse town like Devil's Lake.'

She proffered another genuine smile and with that they set to eating. Two things occurred to him at that juncture.

85

Considering that Angie had just brutally slain her first man, she had handled it very well. There had been no hysteria. If anything she was too calm, too controlled. He would always, to the end of his days, remember his first kill, when he had been forced to gun down a drunken trail hand. Some men just wouldn't listen to sense and back down. Rance had never forgotten the look on his face when the cowman realized that he was dying. He knew that he would have to watch out for Angie, because at some point shock and possibly self-loathing would surely surface.

The other matter was far more mundane, but likely to prove interesting. Neither of them had so far discussed the sleeping arrangements, but then doubtless it would sort itself out. After all, he liked to think of himself as a reasonable man.

7

Rance found himself awake in near total darkness. Something had dragged him out of a deep sleep far earlier than was necessary. He was, of course, lying on the floor but that was not a totally new experience for him. It would take more than just some minor discomfort to rouse him. Hunger wasn't to blame either. His belly was still comfortably full from the late night meal. Then it came to him. The Sharps! What if he were to emerge from the cabin in daylight, just as Jacob Sutter had done two days earlier? If Dan Bodeen just happened to be out there with that damned cannon of his, then the marshal's tenure of the property would be exceedingly short indeed.

Lying very still, he listened to Angie's steady breathing over on the only bed and considered his options. It didn't take him long, because there was really only one that made any sense. Shrugging off the rough woollen blankets, he got to his feet. The stove had cooled down and they had not got around to lighting a proper fire in the hearth, consequently the cabin was now bitterly cold. He smiled grimly at the thought of conditions in the barn.

Armed as ever with his shotgun, he carefully unbarred the door and stepped out. He was reassured by the enveloping inky blackness. He would be invisible to any distant sharpshooter. Not that anyone was likely to be out there. Only very hardy animals could survive in the open at that time of year. By Rance's reckoning it was very probable that Bodeen was at the Barclay cabin, just as he had been two nights before, resting after a kill.

Reaching the barn, he pushed open the door and stepped inside. The road agents' horses moved uneasily at the sound of an interloper. Rance had tied the two men to a large roof support post. With much experience of handling prisoners, he was confident that they would still be there.

'You bastard,' croaked a man's voice, some few paces away.

Moving in close, Rance could just make out the two men lying on the floor.

'You killed him, you son of a bitch!'

If that was true, the marshal had a shrewd idea just who had died and who had endured the fearsome cold. A cursory examination indicated that the consumptive was indeed dead. His heart had probably given out under the terrible ordeal. Shivering now with the intense chill, Rance decided that the sooner he got back inside the cabin the better.

'His death was natural justice,' he remarked drily to the pock marked survivor. 'He certainly won't be missed, whereas you at least get a second chance. You're coming with me. When I slice through the rope, get up slow. Any resistance and you get both barrels.'

As it turned out the man was in no condition to struggle. It took an age for his circulation to return, and even longer for him to stagger over to the cabin. He appeared too stupefied with hypothermia to enquire into the reason for his relocation. Not so Angie, once she discovered his presence.

'What the hell is that piece of trash doing in here?'

She had obviously forgotten her concern of the previous night.

Rance, too cold to argue, answered brusquely. 'Saving our lives. He stays! Now feed that damned stove.'

She did as she was bidden, allowing him to ask one particular question of their so-called guest.

'What's your name, convict?'

That man lay on the floor gasping for breath. Finally he was able to answer. 'Cooper. Zebulon Cooper.'

'Well Zeb,' responded his captor. 'You're going to lie there and stay nice and quiet until morning. Then I've got a job for you.'

Cooper must have been grateful merely to be surviving the night, because he didn't ask what his task might be. Angie too, held her peace. She was beginning to understand just what kind of man Rance Toller was. He appeared undeniably decent and honest, but behind all that lurked a strong ruthless streak. She supposed that no man could survive in his line of work without it. That hard edge was not unattractive, an opinion that would have perked Rance up no end had he only known about it.

* * *

After the night's tribulations, the morning was well advanced before they stirred. Angie headed for the door, carrying one of her prized possessions from back East: a chamber pot.

'Stand fast,' barked Rance. 'No one goes out there just yet.'

'You really wouldn't want me to spill this,' she replied tartly.

91

Without acknowledging her remark, Rance kicked Cooper smartly in the ribs. 'Now's the time to earn your reprieve.'

'Earn my what?' Cooper mumbled, his wits still addled. 'What did he just say?'

'Put this coat and hat on and go empty the piss pot.' So saying, Rance tossed over his own clothes. His pock-marked prisoner stared at him in astonishment. Then the enormity of the order seeped into his befuddled mind.

'I go out there dressed in those duds and likely I'll get shot.'

'There is that chance,' Rance allowed, as he cocked both hammers of his shotgun. 'But if you don't, you definitely will. It's your choice.'

Sufficient light made it through the shutters for him to see the effect of that threat. As Cooper pulled on the heavy coat he whined, 'This just ain't right. You haven't even fed me yet!'

'Tell that to the passengers on the

stage,' Rance retorted as he unbarred the door.

Angie looked on in horror. Was the marshal really intending to send him out to his death? She didn't have to wait long for an answer.

'Pick up the pot,' commanded Rance. 'Slowly walk out a ways, then empty it. When you make it back here, there'll be some hot coffee waiting.'

Cooper picked up the pot gingerly, as though it contained molten metal, very reluctant to pass the threshold. An icy wind blew into the cabin, negating the efforts of the stove.

'Get the hell out there, Zeb.' So saying, Rance prodded him between the shoulder blades with his shotgun.

Cursing fluently, Cooper hesitantly advanced into the bitter morning air. Encouraging words followed him. 'If you try to run for it, I'll cut you down like the dog that you are!'

With that, Rance passed his shotgun to Angie and chambered a round into the Winchester. He knew full well that any premature gunplay was likely to be at a distance. For the second time since fleeing Devil's Lake, he wished that he owned the rifle variant. He momentarily considered switching it for Angie's Henry, but decided against it. Every weapon had its own quirks and now was not the time to be experimenting.

'Do you really think that Bodeen's out there?' asked Angie, mixed emotions playing on her features.

'I would be,' he remarked flatly. 'The real question is how many are with him.'

He wanted to say more, much more to ease her discomfort but time was pressing. Easing open the front window shutter a couple of inches, he watched Cooper trudging through the snow. There was so much open ground before them that Bodeen could have been anywhere.

Watching intently for any movement, he addressed Angie softly. 'If Bodeen believes that it's really me and takes a shot, he will then definitely move in on the cabin. Leaving you alive was a mistake that he won't repeat.'

★   ★   ★

Zebulon Cooper grimaced with distaste as he tipped the night's urine into the pristine snow. The task itself was nothing, but he was effectively a tethered goat awaiting a predator and he didn't like it one bit. Nevertheless, he was beginning to feel a little more confident about the situation. No heavy calibre bullet had struck him as he emerged from that damned cabin. Once he got back in there he'd get some hot coffee and maybe even some bacon. Then he'd look for a way to get clear of that stinking marshal. The man was supposed to be a peace officer, for Christ's sake. He'd got no right setting him up like this.

As he retraced his steps, he noticed the small opening in the shutters of the front window. Miserable bastard's watching me all the time, he thought. Him and that twelve gauge. If he hadn't been there we'd have had some real fun with that little bitch.

It never occurred to him to reflect that that 'little bitch' had very nearly killed him. Moisture dripped off his nose and he reached up to wipe it. The .52 calibre soft lead bullet ploughed into his back with unstoppable force. With no control whatsoever over his movements, Cooper crashed headlong on to the frozen ground. His innards were on fire as he pawed at the snow, desperate for relief. The bloody death that he had avoided for so long was finally upon him, and such was the excruciating pain that he actually welcomed it.

* * *

With frightening clarity, Angie watched as Zebulon Cooper agonizingly clawed his way towards her. His predicament bore a startling similarity to the murder of her husband only two days before, and brought tears streaming from her eyes. How could it all be happening again? Despite her animosity for the outlaw, she found herself willing him on. She even wondered why Rance didn't rush out to help him.

Cooper's head exploded like a ripe melon as another gunshot echoed around the valley. Abruptly all movement ceased. There was no longer a human being out there, just inert flesh and bone. Incredibly the body then jerked under the impact of a third projectile.

'He must think I'm a very dangerous man,' remarked Rance softly.

As though in direct answer, Bodeen's deep voice boomed out in the distance. 'Now you're a dead man, Toller. Ha ha ha!'

The two occupants of the cabin gazed at each other intently. Yet again Rance had been correct in his assessment of events. And another man was dead.

'That bit of bluster was for your benefit,' he informed her. 'To soften you up. He'll move in on the cabin next and try talking you out.'

With that, he switched his gaze back to the gap in the shutters. From then on he kept his eyes firmly on the terrain, talking quietly and with great certainty.

'I figure there'll be five of them including Bodeen. They'll be sure of their numbers and of the effect that my death has had on you. They'll want to disarm you fast. Keep out of sight and do as I tell you. Do you understand?'

Numbly she nodded her acquiescence.

'I said, do you understand?'

'Yes,' she cried out angrily. 'I really don't want any more killing, you know.'

'Tell *them* that,' he replied bitterly. 'All I'm trying to do is keep us both alive.'

There really wasn't anything else to say and so silence descended on the cabin. Angie remained by the open door, rifle in hand. Rance had propped his Winchester against the wall, cocked and ready. The deadly sawn-off shotgun was in his hands again, ready for the expected parley.

For some minutes neither of them saw anything. The ill-fated Zebulon Cooper might just as well have been struck down by lightning. Then the first of the heavily muffled figures came into view. Four others followed him in quick succession. Making no attempt at concealment, all five men began to converge on the cabin.

'This is meant to intimidate you,' hissed Rance. 'Tell them to stay back or you'll fire.'

Angie was actually feeling well and truly intimidated, but she shouted out boldly, 'Stand off, or I'll open up with this repeater!'

The five regulators slowed their approach but kept on coming. Although a thick woollen scarf hid his features, Dan Bodeen was easily recognizable. The single shot Sharps rifle that he clutched represented a potent threat, but one that was negated by the decreasing distance between them. His big mistake, Rance considered, was in not staying well back and leaving his men to say the words.

With about ten yards to go, Bodeen came to a halt. The two men on either side of him also stopped. They knew their business and had avoided bunching up. Bodeen dragged the scarf down and attempted a smile. As usual it entirely failed to reach his eyes.

'It doesn't need to be like this, Mrs Sutter. We just want the land. No one else needs to get hurt. Just throw out your long gun and then follow it. We'll see you safely on a stage with some greenbacks in your purse to help get you situated.'

Angie didn't need any prompting from Rance. She had her reply ready. 'The stagecoach to Grand Forks maybe?'

Bodeen actually displayed genuine amusement at that. 'Ah, so they talked before he killed them. Marshal Toller was very thorough. He must have made some real fancy moves to get the drop on all four of them.'

'Ask him why you should believe him,' hissed Rance.

Hidden behind the open door, she posed the question. Bodeen placed his rifle on the ground and spread his arms wide, as though in supplication.

'You've got no good reason to trust me, lady, and at least one good reason to hate me, but you can believe this: killing a white woman is a sure way to get trouble out here. Why do you think I left you alone two days ago? Now you just heave that smoke pole out here and we can all get warm again.'

'What about my knowledge of the stagecoach hold-up?'

Bodeen chuckled appreciatively before replying. 'Clever little thing, aren't you? Look, you're no threat to me because there are no witnesses. That damned marshal saw to that.'

The damned marshal kept his shot-gun just inside the opening in the shutters and lined up on Bodeen. He would never get a better chance.

The gunhand on Bodeen's extreme left shuffled about in an effort to combat the bitter cold. Idly he glanced over at Cooper's bloody corpse.

'Agree to it,' murmured Rance, momentarily glancing at Angie. It was as he looked through the shutters again that he knew he had overplayed his hand. The gunhand had noticed something wrong about Cooper's body. As his head swung to the right to alert Bodeen, the man jerked up his Winchester so that it was covering the front window.

'Dan, that ain't Toller lying there!'

The time for talking was at an end. Rance had to choose between Bodeen and the gun thug, fast. If he were to blast Bodeen, he would be open to the other man's weapon, which was aimed directly at him. Shifting his aim to cover the most immediate threat, the lawman squeezed one trigger. The murderous discharge caught the man who had discovered his deception square in his chest. That individual's lifeless body collapsed directly on to Bodeen's first victim.

Ignoring the stabbing pain in his right ear, Rance shifted position and fired at the next regulator in line. That man was only slightly luckier. The barrel's contents caught him on the turn, taking him in the left shoulder and throwing him back into the snow. The two powerful detonations in such a confined space had wrought havoc with the marshal's eardrums. Blood was trickling out of his right ear and nausea threatened to overwhelm him. Worst of all, Bodeen and his two compatriots were no longer to be seen.

Angie, having slammed shut and barred the front door, was gazing at him nonplussed. Not surprisingly, she had absolutely no idea what to do next. His head hurt and he could taste bile in the back of his throat, but Rance knew that their survival hung on any decision made by him at that point. 'We're going,' he announced.

Angie gazed at him incredulously. 'Going! Where? Why? This is my home, for Christ's sake!'

Bullets peppered the open front shutter. Keeping low, Rance fired once only for effect. 'It's freezing out there,' he replied. 'There aren't enough of them to rush us and they can't take the time to starve us out. So they'll torch the place and wait on events. We get out through the back, now, while they're getting themselves situated.'

He stared at her intently. 'Believe me, it's the only way.'

Understanding and acceptance registered on her features. She then did something that both surprised and delighted him. Reaching out, she gently touched the side of his face. 'You're bleeding.'

'I think I've burst an eardrum,' he replied. 'I'll survive. Get your gun and anything you can carry.'

She had one more thing to say. 'Take this coat. It was Jacob's. Without it you'll ice over.'

Accepting the heavy garment gladly, he pulled it on. It was definitely oversized, but would suffice. Unbarring the rear shutters, he gently eased them open. The barn was directly facing them and had to be their next destination. The horses and wagon were all inside. Rance knew that that gruesome conveyance definitely could not accompany them any further.

Screened by the cabin, the two fugitives clambered through the window and ran for the large building. They were discovered just on the point of entry. Bullets thwacked into the timber. Angie shrieked as a splinter scored her neck. Blood welled up in the cut but mercifully it was superficial. Anger flared up within her and she snapped off two shots in quick succession. Then together they closed and barred the doors. With his shotgun loaded and ready, Rance knew that the three men would not be in any all-fired hurry to pursue them. He and Angie had open ground around them and plenty of firing points amongst the broken timbers of the barn. Yet sooner or later someone would flank them. Which meant that if they were going to flee yet again it would have to be soon.

'Damn it all,' snapped Rance. 'I'm getting real tired of all this running shit.'

As another bullet slammed into the structure, Angie had her own contribution to make. 'The wagon will slow us down and Jacob would wish to stay here. Do you have any lucifers?'

Rance was stunned but also surreptitiously pleased. 'What do you intend?'

With grim determination etched on her features, Angie stated, 'I mean to fire the barn and everything left in it!'

8

'Do you know what you're saying?' he demanded incredulously. He had only heard her through his undamaged left ear, but it had been enough to gain his total attention.

'My life here is over,' she proclaimed. 'My husband has gone and bad people want my land. Even if we stop these men, others will come. You *know* that!'

As she spoke, more bullets thwacked into the surrounding walls. Bodeen obviously had no intention of just passively awaiting their next move. Even though the pressure on them both was mounting, Rance took the time to observe her closely. He witnessed the determination in her eyes, the firm set to her features and most of all the way her lips moved as she sealed the fate of her property. Despite the dire situation, he was entranced.

'So will you help me?'

It seemed to him that he had heard that question a lot since she had come into his life, but there could really only be one possible response. Nodding gravely, he said, 'You unharness the team and saddle the best for yourself. We'll drive the others out before us. It worked well enough in town.'

As Angie had earlier surmised, the road agents had conveniently tethered their mounts under her roof. There was no time for finesse. The leather traces had to be cut. As she set to work, Rance rapidly pumped and fired his Winchester through a knothole. He hit no one, but his action served to keep heads down.

'Over by the back wall,' Angie called urgently. 'Kerosene in a big jar.'

'That'll answer,' murmured Rance half to himself, as he scrambled to retrieve it.

Liquid kerosene used to fuel the ubiquitous table lamp was, when diluted with the cheaper benzene, highly inflammable. It was just the stuff needed to get the barn burning. Locating the heavy earthenware jar, Rance proceeded to splash the pungent fluid over the rear wall, where the bulk of the hay was to be found. The big jar had been filled for winter, so he had plenty to go at. Such was his endeavour that he didn't even glance at the corpse of the consumptive outlaw still tied to a support post.

Rance kept his precious lucifers wrapped in an oilskin pouch. As one of them flared into life, he tentatively dropped it onto the hay. The result was an instantaneous inferno. Flames spread rapidly onto the rear wall and suddenly it wasn't cold anymore.

Angie had cut loose the horses and saddled her own mount. Disconcerted by the conflagration, the rest of the animals were milling around near the doors.

'This is going to spread fast,' he called over to her. 'Let's get those doors open and skedaddle.'

Angie had one thing left to do. The young widow needed a final look at her husband's body. Somehow she just couldn't acknowledge that she was to be irrevocably separated from him. With her back now hot from the blazing timbers, she walked slowly towards the back of her wagon. She vaguely registered Rance sheathing his Winchester before moving over to the doors. The sudden vicelike grip on her ankle seemed to come from nowhere. Before Angie could even look down, she was brutally wrenched off her feet. A clammy hand reached over her mouth stifling a shriek.

'Going to leave me to burn to death, weren't you, bitch?'

The face that loomed over her was cadaverous. It held the look of a consumptive. But surely he was dead? Then her knife was abruptly in his grasp and she found herself in fear for her own life. Terror gave her strength and she viciously sank her teeth into the man's hand. With an anguished howl he yanked it away, but his other still contained her knife.

'Rance,' she screamed out.

The lawman turned in surprise. He had not expected a challenge from that direction, but, drawing on years of experience, immediately summed up the situation. Professionalism overcame both his fear for her and the anger he felt at not having confirmed beyond all doubt the death of the road agent. Strange thumping noises came from outside the doors, but that would have to wait. Cautiously he advanced on the unhappy couple lying behind the wagon. His shotgun had no place in this new confrontation, so he transferred it to his left hand and drew his revolver. The scrawny outlaw held her in a gruesome embrace. Somehow he had partially freed himself, but his feet were still tethered to the post. He had had to bide his time. Angie's sentimental visit to the wagon had given him his opportunity. Despite being bitten, he still had a blade digging into her neck hard enough to draw blood.

'That's close enough, law dog! You cock that Remington and I'll slice her pretty throat real bad.'

'You know your weapons,' replied Rance smoothly as he tried to figure out just what the hell to do. 'You've also got a surprisingly strong constitution. Few men could have survived out here last night.'

'Don't try that sweet-talking shit,' spat the other man. 'I just want out of here. Holster that piece and cut the damn rope. You try anything, any little thing at all and she's chopped meat.'

As though emphasizing his serious intent, he pressed down on the cutting edge. Angie moaned in pain. Fierce anger surged through the marshal but he forced himself to maintain a calm tone.

'Fair enough, mister. Just ease off on that cutting tool and I'll soon have you free.'

Slowly he lowered his handgun. He had no intention of holstering it. The presence of his weapon was the only thing keeping her alive. All he needed was for the lunger to reduce the pressure. The blow to his left arm took everybody by surprise. The gunshot at the front of the barn coincided with a flash of agony in his upper arm. The heavy shotgun fell to the ground and it was all he could do to remain on his feet. Well, nearly all.

Angie's captor appeared stunned by the sudden development, allowing Rance the opening that he needed. Swiftly cocking and raising his revolver, he took rapid aim. There could only be time for one lethal headshot. With a crash, his gun discharged and the outlaw's left cheekbone seemed to implode. Blood sprayed over Angie and the nearest wagon wheel. The deadly knife fell from nerveless fingers and that particular crisis was abruptly over. Another shot rang out from behind Rance as the noise of a bee in flight passed by his left ear.

That's some wild shooting, he

thought as he holstered his smoking Remington. Grabbing his shotgun, he searched desperately for the bullet's source, whilst at the same time bellowing at Angie. 'Get those bloody doors open. We're going to fry in here.'

The fire had well and truly caught on the rear wall. Flames were shooting up to the roof and the heat was intense. Then he saw the rifle barrel. It was protruding through the same knothole that he had used earlier. The restriction on free movement that it allowed explained why he was still alive. Awkwardly cocking his shotgun, he aimed and fired. The single blast peppered the area around the hole in the wall. From beyond it there came a strident yell and the weapon abruptly disappeared.

Rance's head was throbbing. His ears hurt and he could feel blood trickling down his left arm. Above him the roof timbers were crackling as flames engulfed them. Despite the terrible heat, he just wanted to sit down and rest but that was not an option. Angie's shrill voice carried over the noise of the fire.

'The devils have blocked the doors. I can't open them.'

With a sigh, Rance reloaded the shotgun and moved to join her. Tongues of flame were now spreading to the side walls, so that the whole structure would soon be overwhelmed. Horses plunged around in sheer terror at the front of building. It occurred to him that he and Angie could quite possibly be the first people to burn to death in the middle of winter in the whole of Dakota Territory.

Angie turned as he joined her. She scrutinized him carefully. Although aware that she too was now liberally spattered with blood, she decided that the lawman did not look too good. There was dried blood below his right ear and unknown damage to his left arm. He had very probably just saved her life, yet they were now likely to be cremated together along with her dead husband. It was just not fair.

'There's something heavy wedged against them,' she explained. 'Let's try together.'

Simultaneously Rance and Angie heaved against the heavy doors but they would not budge. Tears of frustration sprang into her eyes. 'If only Jacob had constructed the doors to open inwards,' she shouted irrelevantly.

'Well he didn't,' responded the pragmatic marshal. 'So we'll have to smash our way out. Help me with that wagon.'

From outside there came Bodeen's familiar voice. 'Looks like you're finally going to burn in hell, Toller! You were good, I'll give you that.'

'He just doesn't know when to hush up,' gasped Rance as they reached the conveyance. The inferno around them seemed to be consuming the very air. 'Get the brake off.'

'Not with Jacob in it!'

'Say what?'

'He stays in here,' she replied with

fierce determination. 'It's what he would have wanted.'

There was simply no time to argue. Taking hold of a large booted foot, he indicated that she should do the same. Together they dragged the heavy body off the flatbed and on to the earth. Jacob's head thwacked on the edge as he came down.

'We ain't got time for any fine words,' hollered Rance above the roaring conflagration. 'And Barclay stays put, so get shoving!'

As Angie joined him, he lined up the doors and placed his right shoulder against the back of the wagon. Heaving with all their strength, they got it moving. Unfortunately they could not push *and* steer. The wagon smacked into the right-hand door, partially forcing it open, but then remained wedged in the gap. Cold clear air was visible beyond and drove the trapped horses wild. Careering around, they reared up at the wagon but could not escape.

Angie wanted to cry. Fear and frustration were simultaneously working on her. Rance stood motionless as though in shock. Surely he's not given up, she thought.

One thing was very apparent. All gunfire from outside the barn had ceased. Bodeen and his remaining cronies were obviously enjoying the spectacle and waiting on events. Fire had spread to the whole roof. Her hair was scorching and it was becoming hard to breathe.

'Get under the wagon,' bellowed Rance. He had suddenly appeared at her side with a mallet in his hand. His two long guns were cradled in his left arm. While she had been contemplating death, he had been thinking ahead.

Together they crawled under the wagon bed. Mercifully the air was cooler and fresher down there. Rance pushed the two weapons towards her. 'After this I'll never complain about the cold again. When those skunks see what I'm about, they'll get to firing again.

You blast away with this lot and keep their heads down. I'm going to free up this other door.'

Bodeen had wedged two fence posts up against each door. Tackled from the outside, they would be easy to remove. The only danger was hot lead, especially that from a certain Sharps rifle. As Rance edged into the open, Angie opened up with her Henry. Rapidly working the under-lever, she fired on a broad front.

Rance's left arm ached abominably, but he hammered at the first post like a man possessed. He was under no illusions that this was their last chance. By alternately striking it from each side, he managed to work it loose in the ground. Dragging it out, he threw it to one side and tackled the second one. A steady stream of gunfire came from under the wagon. Then a bullet slammed into the door mere inches from his head. There were at least three men out there, and she couldn't cover them all. With manic energy, he pounded at the final post. If he hadn't shifted it by the time she needed to reload the repeaters, then he would surely be a dead man.

'Nearly out,' Angie yelled up at him.

Heaving the post away, he dropped panting and sweating to the ground and crawled under the wagon to join her.

'That was some real fancy shooting,' he gasped.

Any reply that she might have made was lost in a veritable hail of lead. With a tremendous crack, one of the wheel spokes shattered.

'That damned Sharps again,' Rance muttered. 'Come on.'

Together they crept back into the inferno. They discovered horses that were beside themselves with fear. The humans callously required those creatures that they did not intend to ride, to provide cover. Therefore they couldn't afford to open the left hand door until they were both mounted. As though sensing a way out, two animals allowed their riders to climb into the saddles.

Manoeuvring side on, Rance kicked out sharply at the door. As though by divine providence it swung open smoothly on its hinges. At that point any slight control was lost. All the horses stampeded out of the doomed structure.

Sitting astride a powerful animal in full flight was an exhilarating experience after the extreme anxiety of being trapped in a burning barn. Rapid gunfire pursued them as they fled, but it couldn't detract from the feeling of newfound freedom. Yet even then, with one hand gripping the reins and the other his shotgun, Rance's mind was turning over their options.

'Head towards town,' he bellowed at Angie.

Unable to acknowledge, she just did as he asked. Risking a quick look behind them, the marshal spotted one horse lying on its side, kicking out helplessly. Doubtless the regulators had fired indiscriminately, desperate to bring down the troublesome lawman.

Gradually, as the total chaos receded into the background, they were able to bring their mounts under control. Slowing his panting beast down to a walk, Rance scrutinized their back trail. Heavy smoke was visible across the snowy wasteland, but they were effectively out of sight to Bodeen and his men.

Angie reined in next to him. Her bloodied features were flushed from a punishing combination of fierce heat and extreme cold. He noticed a blister on her lip. That'll hurt later, he decided.

She in turn appraised the lawman. Although bloodstained and dirty, he somehow appeared to be holding up reasonably well, considering all that had befallen him. Yet his left arm was an unknown quantity and would need looking at soon.

'What now?' she asked. It occurred to her that she constantly followed his lead. No man, including her late husband, had ever attained that level of control over her. Perhaps it was because

Rance always seemed to be in the right. That was doubtless true, but there was possibly more to it than that.

'First, we reload the weapons. Then we double back and steal ourselves some horses. Leaving those sons of bitches afoot will give us time to rest up in Devil's Lake. Even if they do manage to catch up with the other runaways, it'll take them plenty of time.'

Despite the situation, Angie could not hide a broad smile. 'You really do have it all thought out, don't you?'

Feeding cartridges into the loading gate of his Winchester, Rance chose to answer in all seriousness. 'I haven't always been marshal of a sleepy little settlement. Some of those big cow towns could be awful hard on a lawman.' Then he favoured her with a slow smile. 'Leastways Devil's Lake used to be sleepy!'

9 *

Marshal Toller knew exactly where to find Dan Bodeen's diminutive horse herd. Most people, even highly dangerous men, tend to be creatures of habit. Bodeen had earlier discovered a convenient location from where to back shoot Jacob Sutter. It seemed highly likely therefore, that he would return there with his four gun thugs to conceal their horses and plan their assault on the cabin. Yet if Rance and Angie were to seize his transport they would need to move fast, before the regulators could return on foot. The real question was, were the animals under guard?

The two horse thieves lay flat in the snow. Below them, in the large hollow, waited five tethered mounts. Their three surviving owners were visible in the distance, backlit by a huge soaring sheet of flame that marked all that remained of the barn. The men were slowly trudging back from Angie's farmhouse. That too was now on fire. Bodeen had obviously decided to prevent any possible reoccupation. Tears of anger and grief now sprang into Angie's eyes. Everything that she had possessed was irrevocably gone.

Silently she lined her Henry up on the distant figures. Without a word, Rance pressed the muzzle down into the snow and emphatically shook his head. There was a more immediate concern. Motioning her back below the crest, he then whispered in her ear. 'We need the horses now. The only way to flush out a guard quickly is for you to break cover. Are you up for it?'

The lawman deeply regretted exposing her to more danger, but, as in marriage they were now both deeply committed, for better or worse.

'Yes,' she replied without hesitation. 'Just don't miss!'

With that, she crawled a few feet away before calmly rising up from the snow. Carefully clambering down the slope, she made straight for the horses. Rance had eased back up to the crest, Winchester at the ready. With both friend and possible foe in front of him, a shotgun was definitely not the weapon of choice.

The battered and bloodied regulator emerged from a clutch of trees. After receiving a fearful quantity of shot in his left shoulder, the hired gun had fashioned a makeshift sling and painfully retreated to where the horses were picketed. He'd had enough gunplay for one day. If Bodeen wanted to mix it with that damned marshal that was up to him. Continued firing suggested that things were not going well. There had then been a period of silence before, lo and behold, the Sutter bitch suddenly appeared out of nowhere before him. No longer capable of two-handed action, the man drew and cocked his Schofield revolver. Knowing that his exacting leader preferred to have the woman alive, he reluctantly held his fire.

Alerted by the metallic click, Angie froze in dismay at the sight of the bloodstained gunman. When agreeing to act as live bait, she hadn't really believed that she would actually confront anyone.

'Lose the Henry,' ordered the gunman coldly.

At that moment Rance rose up on the rim, aimed directly at the man's torso and fired. There was a loud metallic click and then . . . silence. *Misfire!*

Horrified at the lawman's sudden appearance, his prey twisted to his right and took rapid aim. The pain and stiffness induced by his multiple wounds conspired to slow his reactions. As the gunman fired, Rance dropped back out of sight into the snow and levered out the defective cartridge. There was another loud report from the hollow, only now it came from a rifle. Rolling once to his right, Rance again levelled his Winchester. This time his doubtful assistance was not needed. Below him lay the regulator, fresh blood pumping from a fatal chest wound.

As the luckless gunman jerked and twitched in his death throes, Angie began to tremble violently. Her eyes widened like saucers as she stared at the dying man. She had seen many men gunned down in recent days, but this was the second by her own hand. For some reason that she could not comprehend, hysteria threatened to take hold of her, but was prevented by the arrival of yet another threat.

From the direction of her blazing cabin came angry cries, followed by more shots. Rance bellowed out, 'Get back up here, *now!*'

There was a slapping sound as a bullet hit the snow nearby. They didn't have long. Bodeen and his two remaining men were running towards them. It was no longer possible to simply steal the horses. As Angie hurriedly clambered out of the hollow, the peace officer hardened his heart. Pulling the butt tightly into his shoulder, he rapidly fired and pumped the lever action of his carbine five times. There were no more misfires.

The mayhem below him was quite appalling. Five horses lay stricken, kicking out and screaming in an almost human fashion. His face ashen, Rance turned away and grabbed Angie by the arm. Wordlessly, he propelled her towards their own horses.

'What have you done?' she cried out. 'They're still alive!'

'The only thing I could do,' he snarled, heaving her up into the saddle. 'This isn't some sort of game. Those bastards have got to get past five thrashing animals now.'

Wincing from the pain in his left arm, Rance mounted up and urged his horse into motion. As they left the carnage behind, Dan Bodeen's deep voice followed after them.

'You'll pay for this, Toller. Mark my words!'

Briefly turning to glance at Angie's strained features, Rance called over,

'Well at least he doesn't just want me dead now.'

* * *

The journey back to town across the freezing terrain was a distinctly sombre one. Both of them had reasons to brood. Rance held the slaughter of innocent animals to be a far crueller deed than the killing of any number of hired guns. Unfortunately, and to his certain knowledge, it was nothing new in the bloody history of the American West. In 1874 during the army's campaign against the Comanches, Colonel Mackenzie's Fourth Cavalry Troopers had captured and shot over a thousand horses in one day. It had very effectively curtailed the raider's savage depredations, but that didn't make it right.

With a conscious effort, Rance emerged from his dark thoughts and gazed over at Angie. The second fatal shooting had deeply affected her. Realizing that he had to say something to try and ease her pain or at least show that he understood it, he edged his horse closer to hers.

'If you should need a shoulder to cry on, mine's as good as anyone's. It's a terrible thing to take a man's life, but the hurt lessens with each one. And they did need killing.'

Favouring him with a sad smile she asked, 'Does there have to be any more? We could just leave Devil's Lake to its gold and its greed and move on. There's nothing left for me here.'

Rance's heart pounded. Had she just said 'we'? The thought of accompanying Angie anywhere held great appeal for him. Unfortunately he had some pressing unfinished business. Returning her smile he replied, 'Right now I'm the only law in Devil's Lake and I'm all through with running. Bodeen and his crew are answerable for at least three murders. He's going to keep coming and when he does I'll be waiting. After that, well, it'll be up to the town to decide if they still want a marshal.'

Angie regarded him steadily for some moments. Then she reached out and patted his right arm. 'You're a real push hard, aren't you, Marshal Toller?'

'Not so as you'd notice, ma'am,' he replied in a bantering tone.

Angie responded with a broad smile and a gay laugh. Rance had not witnessed either before, and for him the transformation was quite miraculous. To his jaded eyes, she looked simply delectable. The effect was sufficient to actually make him forget the persistent throbbing in his left arm. Things were definitely looking up.

10

Despite the punishing cold, Dan Bodeen was dangerously close to boiling point. Sheer incandescent rage had been slowly building inside him ever since his totally unexpected arrest two days earlier in Pearsall's. To be unceremoniously packed off to jail by a two-bit law dog had been hard to swallow. Having to carry his own foul-smelling hired hand had only added grist to the mill. Since then he had consistently underestimated his opponent and, as a consequence, had been outsmarted at every turn. His mission to gain effective control of the Devil's Lake area was being jeopardized by one man. It would not, could not, stand!

He was finally shaken out of his bitter self-recrimination by Seth's hesitant call. 'What would you have us do with the livestock, boss?'

With Toller and the Sutter bitch long gone, the three men no longer had any need to get past the thrashing animals. Each one was severely wounded and incapable of carrying a man. Their pitiful crying had left Bodeen untouched, but he did acknowledge that the constant noise was getting on his frayed nerves.

'Kill them all,' he snarled back. 'Hell, the way this trip's headed, we might just end up eating them.'

His sour jest held an uncomfortable truth. The terrified horses from the burning barn had fled at a tremendous rate and were probably still running. Therefore the three men faced a long walk back to town, which was unlikely to be accomplished before darkness set in. Arriving there tired and on foot would leave them vulnerable to any action by that damned marshal — all supposing that they didn't freeze to death first. Also, having left Devil's Lake in hot pursuit, they had virtually no food. The fact that they had just burned down their closest source of shelter only added to Bodeen's inner turmoil.

In the fifteen years since the surrender at Appomattox, he had honed the lethal skills gained in the Army of Northern Virginia by working as a hired gun. Over that period, he had learned to control the burning resentment gained from having been on the losing side, but the anger never left him. One thing he had discovered early on in that damned war was never to indulge in gunplay before thoroughly scrutinizing your surroundings. Drawing in a deep breath, the regulators' leader forced himself to think rationally. Raising his right hand he called out, 'Hold fast.' Then, removing a drawtube spyglass from his pocket, he carefully scanned the frozen wasteland that surrounded him. Plumes of smoke were still rising from the two destroyed buildings. Since Indians had ceased to be a threat in the region, it was likely that anybody witnessing them would investigate. And sure enough, way back up the valley beyond the Sutter place, he spotted a little clutch of black dots.

Smiling grimly at his two waiting men, he remarked, 'Best use a cutting tool, boys. Likely we'll have visitors before long. Wouldn't want gunfire to put them off.'

* * *

The scavengers had spotted the twin smoke spirals from miles back. Like all such creatures they operated with great caution. Smoke meant people. People meant goods and chattels, but also danger. Anyone familiar with the flotsam and jetsam of the frontier would have felt no surprise at humans being referred to as scavengers. It perfectly suited the character of the five men viewing the remains of Angie Sutter's homestead. All of them were gaunt and unkempt. Pickings had been cruelly lacking and desperation showed in their eyes. The leader of the horsemen, Cole Dekker, surveyed the scene with great suspicion.

'Not long past, wreckage like that would have smelt of Indian trouble,' he remarked dolefully. 'But those days are gone. Leastways in these parts.'

'Praise the Lord for that,' replied the individual on his right. 'Those dirt-worshipping heathens cast a blight over this land for long enough.'

Known only as the Preacher, his benign and sober appearance concealed a vicious temperament that had claimed many lives. His righteous words drew grunts of agreement from the other three mounted men. Concealed under layers of frayed and grubby clothing, all were dissolute dangerous men. They had no words of wisdom to impart, since in truth they possessed very little intelligence. It was sufficient that they did as they were told. They remained with Dekker because he usually managed to put food in their mouths and provide cartridges for their outdated weaponry. It was lack of the former that finally pushed Dekker into making a fateful decision. Times had been far too lean recently.

'We can sit up here all day, but it ain't going to put food in our bellies. Let's ease on down there, boys.'

So saying, he led his men down carefully towards the smoking ruins. Long experience had taught the lawless band to spread out and use every bit of cover. Unfortunately, the deck was already stacked against them. A more dangerous predator had got their measure.

★   ★   ★

'I want at least one squealer,' murmured Bodeen, as he adjusted the ladder sight on his Sharps rifle. 'No one in their right mind would be travelling in this weather without good reason. I want to know what that reason is. I want to know what's brought them to this godforsaken spot at this particular time.'

The three men were concealed in deep snow, about a hundred yards from Angie's ruined home. Seth lay on Bodeen's right, whilst the other man, Charlie Portis, was on his left. They were both armed with the latest Model 1876 .45-.75 Winchesters. Far stronger and more powerful than the earlier models, they made excellent man-stoppers. Although the five strangers were getting closer, the regulators' leader continued to observe them through his spyglass. Two of them appeared to be deliberately hanging back, as though using the others as cover.

Sensible move, considered Bodeen, who had done the same thing himself many times. *And* there was something about them that seemed familiar.

'I reckon I know the two at the back,' he whispered. 'We'll drop the other three and then see what happens. *Don't* hit the horses.'

His two men remained silent. They knew what was expected of them and took no pleasure in idle chitchat with their leader. He seemed to permanently exude an aura of menace, which even they found off-putting.

At fifty yards the newcomers were, had they only known it, dead meat. With powerful rifles in the hands of professionals achieving total surprise, the outcome could never have been in doubt. By pre-arrangement, Bodeen fired his Sharps first. With a roar the heavy calibre bullet sped down the thirty inch barrel and on unerringly to its target. His prey was blasted backwards off his horse and left twitching helplessly on the ground. Fresh blood coated the virgin snow. As the other two fired, he calmly retracted the hammer to safety and load and levered down the falling block. Even as he slipped in another cartridge, he dispassionately observed two more dead men hit the ground.

Dekker and the Preacher did exactly what was expected of them. They dismounted rapidly and dropped to the frozen ground. Both of them had recognized the sound of the Sharps. There was no outrunning one of those. As its owner clambered cautiously to his feet, Dekker thought, Christ, I know that face.

Bodeen advanced calmly and deliberately, his rifle muzzle hovering somewhere between the two prone survivors. 'Looks to me like you're kind of outmatched,' he commented mildly. 'You can burrow into that snow all you want, but you'll still get blown all to hell. *Or* you can work for me. I know you, Dekker, you'll do anything for a few greenbacks. What'll it be?'

Dekker looked questioningly at his companion. The Preacher shrugged as he quietly responded, 'That son of a bitch would kill his own mother. Come to think of it, I think he did. *But* I'm powerful hungry and we ain't got a dime between us.'

Dekker nodded his understanding. Turning back to Bodeen, he called out, 'Seems like the least we can do is talk about it.'

* * *

The five men stood in front of Angie's smouldering barn. The heat was no longer overwhelming; in fact it was downright comforting on such a bitter day. Seth and Charlie had recovered the three riderless horses. The grim prospect of a gruelling walk back to Devil's Lake had gone. Bodeen slowly looked Dekker and the Preacher up and down.

'You know,' he remarked conversationally, 'I really can't recall it ever being as cold as this. You'd need a real good reason to travel. Just what brings you to these parts?'

Dekker eyed him cautiously. There really didn't seem much point in lying. 'We heard rumours about a gold strike. Thought we might get lucky at last.'

'Or maybe take it off someone who had,' laughed Bodeen. As usual with him there was little sign of good humour. 'You two don't look too prosperous,' he continued. 'How would you like to earn some real money?

Money that doesn't have to be tin panned or stolen.'

'I'll allow that we could use a little currency, friend.' The Preacher rubbed his hands together as though in anticipation. 'Just what kind of work were you thinking of?'

Bodeen scratched his whiskery face. There'd been little time for shaving recently. 'There's a marshal, name of Toller. Carries the law in Devil's Lake. He's all on his lonesome and I want him in the ground. You two do that for me and you're on regular wages, and maybe even a bonus.'

Dekker nodded encouragingly, expecting some elaboration, but none came. That was it. Kill some unknown lawman, or die there and then. He looked over at his companion. The other man just shrugged. 'Damn little use he is,' he considered. 'What the hell, let's do it!'

'Never did care for the law,' he remarked. 'This tin star, what's he look like?'

'Just under six foot. Early forties. Fair hair. He doesn't favour a beard or moustache and he always keeps a sawn-off with him.'

Dekker began to get the picture. Bodeen and his pistoleers had already tried. Regarding the regulator steadily, he asked, 'You reckon an old Spencer and a Trapdoor Springfield is enough to put him down?'

Favouring the other man with a speculative gaze, Bodeen came to a rapid decision. He just happened to have some surplus weapons, whose owners no longer had a use for them.

'Seth, Charlie, give them the spare Winchesters. Lever out a full load. No spare cartridges.'

His two gunnies bristled with indignation, but both knew better than to protest. Reluctantly they emptied the rifles, and then handed them and the cartridges to Dekker and the Preacher.

'How do we get paid?' queried Dekker, as he appraised his new weapon. 'When we've butchered your friend the law dog?'

'We're fixing to get into town tomorrow,' Bodeen replied. 'I've got more riders coming. You'll get what's coming to you then.'

The two scavengers exchanged guarded glances, but made no further comment. Mounting up, they slowly moved off through the snow, away from the smoking buildings. Although used to the smell of death, they were nonetheless glad to be going.

Bodeen called after them, 'If you get lucky, I might even be able to put myself up for marshal, ha, ha.' Then in an aside to his men, he remarked, 'If either of them reloads, kill them both!'

★   ★   ★

The Preacher had a splendid idea. 'Why don't we load these fine new Winchesters and parole them all to Jesus?'

Dekker regarded him pityingly. 'That Truthful Sharps would have you face down before you got the first cartridge through the loading gate. Besides, if we do get lucky with this tin star, we might just be on fighting wages for a change. Wouldn't that be something?'

His companion regarded him dubiously. 'I suppose. All the same, it was a shame about the other three.'

'Three what?'

11

Darkness fell unpleasantly early at that time of year, yet some good can come out of anything. Its onset afforded Rance and Angie the opportunity to get round the back of the livery without being noticed. Tethering their animals near the rear wall, the marshal handed his Winchester to his new deputy. Cruelly, it occurred to him that she certainly had the edge on Clem in looks.

They silently made their way along the side of the building. The main street was empty of people, but from the direction of Pearsall's Emporium came a deal of raucous laughter. 'Good to know somebody's having some fun,' whispered Rance.

With the arrival of dusk, Silas had closed the main doors but the small access door contained within one of them was always unlocked. The two peace officers entered swiftly and scanned the interior. The stalls held many animals, as expected at that time of year, but none showed any obvious signs of recent hard riding. Of Silas there was no sign, but his black stable hand ventured towards them.

Middle-aged with prematurely white hair, the man had worked for Silas for at least as long as Rance had been in Devil's Lake. No one knew where he'd come from. He had just appeared one day, seeking work. It was rumoured that he had been a plantation slave, freed by the Union Army's bayonets, but then again he could quite easily have been a runaway. Such things mattered little to folks in the extreme north of the United States.

He greeted them both politely but without a trace of subservience. 'Good evening, Marshal, ma'am. Mr Silas ain't likely to be long. You're both welcome to wait.'

'I intend to,' replied Rance shortly. To

Angie, he said, 'You stay here please.'

Something about his instinctive assumption of authority suddenly riled her out of all proportion to what had really just been a simple request. Just who does he think he is? she fumed silently. Before he could make a move, she prodded him sharply in the chest.

'If you're through giving orders, I've got one for you. In case you've forgotten, you're wounded. If it doesn't get looked at it'll fester and gangrene will set in. Then you'll likely lose the arm and be no use to anybody!'

Taken by surprise, he viewed her silently for a moment. It occurred to him that she was quite a firebrand and all the more desirable because of it. She also happened to be spot on. He sighed and proffered a weary smile.

'You're quite right and I appreciate your concern. I really do. Trouble is, I must find out who we're up against in town. If anybody catches me unawares, then we're both finished.' Brushing his hand lightly against her cheek he concluded with, 'And I really don't want that.'

Then he casually strolled back to the door and took up station next to it. The stablehand glanced at him curiously before returning to his tasks. Hard experience had taught him to mind his own business. Angie, on the other hand, stared at him with far more than just simple curiosity.

As it turned out, they didn't have long to wait. Rance had barely got situated, before the small door opened and Silas's spare frame eased through. As he caught sight of Angie, his unshaven features registered puzzlement. That was soon replaced by unease as he glanced over his shoulder.

'Hello, Silas,' said the marshal softly. 'You look surprised to see me.'

The other man swallowed painfully as he searched for the right words. 'Ha, yes, well. I did just wonder what had become of you after you quit town yesterday.'

'There's been a lot of dying since

then,' responded Rance flatly. 'Oh, and you were right about the Grand Forks Stage. It was road agents. They were working for your new friends.'

That was all too much for the livery owner. His legs seemed to buckle and suddenly he found himself sitting on the cold hard ground. Appearing terminally dazed, he looked from Rance to Angie and back again. With a display of supreme contempt etched on his features, the marshal strolled over to him.

'How many of these so-called regulators are left in town?'

Peering up at his inquisitor, Silas tried to pull himself together. 'Four or five, I guess. They're all over at Pearsall's supping joy juice. Bodeen rides them kind of hard, so with him out chasing you two all over God's creation they thought to have a celebration.'

He giggled nervously at the realization of what he had just said. Seeing the hard set in Rance's eyes, he tried again.

'There's more coming though, soon.'

The lawman didn't ask how he knew, because he didn't really care. Silas was about to receive some instructions and God help him if he didn't comply.

'We're going to have us a town meeting. You're going to find Jered Tonks, Tom Brennan and, of course, the minister. Bring them all here.'

Silas struggled to his feet. 'What do I tell them?'

'Tell them anything you want. Just get them,' was Rance's unhelpful reply. 'Because if you don't, I'll burn this livery down around your shoulders. It won't be the first today!'

Its owner turned ashen. He appeared about to protest but thought better of it and headed for the door. Rance's next course of action was clear, at least to him. Turning to face Angie, he consciously relaxed his features. He knew that he had to take advantage of her trust once again and he didn't like it one bit.

'I intend visiting Pearsall's. Any man

I find packing a gun will be arrested.'

Angie favoured him with a tense smile as she replied, 'And you want me to back your play.'

That drew a genuine laugh from the lawman. She was even beginning to sound like a deputy. Gently taking her arm, he led her towards the nearest empty stable. It was about to double as a boudoir.

'Actually,' he remarked jovially, 'I want you to get rid of that huge coat, tighten your belt and let your hair down. You're going to a party.'

* * *

And what a party it turned out to be. Peering through a corner window into the saloon, Angie could discern a number of men moving about. Even though the poor quality glass was heavily distorted, she could tell that some of them were wearing not much more than their long johns. That seemed to be a regular occurrence in her life recently. High-pitched shrieking also indicated that there were a number of Dutch gals present. None of which was likely to make her necessarily dramatic entrance any easier.

Viewed from outside, the flickering oil lamps endowed the large room with a welcoming feel that she knew would be illusory. Shivering with cold, she decided that Rance had had enough time to get into position in the saloon's back room. At his insistence, she had reluctantly discarded the thick coat and released her sandy hair from its bonds. Even though she wasn't covered in rouge, she knew from the way men had regarded her in the past that she was tolerably attractive. Now was the time to put it to the test.

The door glass rattled in its frame as Angie twisted the handle and pushed against the swollen wood. Clutching her rifle, she stepped into the smoky room and waited for someone to take notice. That took longer than she had antici-pated. Although the night was still young, the drinking was well advanced. As her gaze took in the interior, Angie realized that she had stumbled into a purely private shindig: its only participants were Bodeen's trash and an assortment of hookers, so called because of Union General 'fighting Joe' Hooker's renowned weakness for prostitutes. One of them was so far gone, as to be sprawled on the bar with her ample breasts displayed for all to see.

It was Jed, the saloonkeeper, who finally became aware of her presence. He was a grey-haired, unshaven, unsavoury individual who looked perfectly suited to his surroundings. Raising his bushy eyebrows in surprise, he called over to her, 'What can we do for you, little lady? Don't be shy. Come on in.'

As she absorbed his condescending greeting, two things occurred. Bodeen's men finally focused on her and Angie began to get angry. Raising the muzzle to waist height, she chambered a round into the Henry. Trying her best to at least sound like a peace officer, she called out, 'Drop your weapons and line up by the bar.'

Even a room full of drunkards cannot long ignore a pretty woman holding a loaded gun. Angie's wrath was then suddenly tempered by the realization that she now definitely had everybody's attention. *And,* just as the night before, she found herself desperately wondering just where the hell Rance had got to. One of the men, a huge bearded pistoleer, lumbered to his feet. Drunkenly bowing from the waist, he leered over at her. 'You don't need no long gun to get my attention, darling.'

His *compadres* were staring fixedly at her, their lurking whores temporarily forgotten. To Angie, it felt as though the temperature in the room had suddenly risen by many degrees. Sweat began to form in her armpits and under her breasts. Cocking her rifle, she aimed it directly at the hulking spokesman.

'Last warning,' she spat back. 'Drop them!'

'Pants or pieces?' the big man

guffawed. The others all laughed appreciatively, but the humour noticeably failed to reach their bloodshot eyes. One of them licked his lips as he mentally undressed the new deputy.

Stepping carefully out of the storeroom, Rance smiled grimly at the backs of the assembled regulators. Thanks to Angie's melodramatic arrival, they were exactly where he wanted them. Like lambs to the slaughter.

A painted lady, her dubious charms forgotten, glanced over at him and froze in shock. The town marshal winked at her at he calmly pointed his Remington at the ceiling and fired. In the relatively quiet room the sudden discharge was shattering. Rapidly holstering his revolver, Rance took a two handed grip on the deadly sawn-off. As the assembled shootists lurched round in surprise, he stated, 'Ease off, boys. The next one won't be in the roof. Now do as the lady said and drop those belt irons.'

In truth only two of the men wore

gunbelts. The others had discarded them along with their trousers, as a preliminary to the expected lovemaking. The great oaf who had taunted Angie just happened to be one of those still carrying a gun and he was in no hurry to surrender it. Fuelled by alcohol, he slowly looked the marshal up and down.

'The great Rance Toller. You don't look so tough to me. You're just some worn-out tin star living off a reputation.'

So saying, he began to ease his right hand towards the butt of his revolver. His cronies, mistakenly sensing fear in Rance's silence, began to close in. Just as they had with Angie.

Coolly lowering the muzzles of his big gun, the lawman squeezed one trigger. The piece discharged with a deafening roar. The pain in his remaining eardrum was nothing compared to that inflicted on the man before him. The load of shot took the gunhand in both legs centred on the

158

knees. With a howl of pure agony, that man collapsed to the floor. He lay there jerking, twitching and crying out for his mother, all bravado irrevocably gone.

'Aw, shut up,' remarked Rance dismissively.

As a great cloud of sulphurous smoke drifted towards the ceiling, three of his four companions backed off. The fourth, foolishly undaunted by the carnage, stood his ground. He was a thickset man in his twenties, too young to have served in the War Between the States but nonetheless hardened to violence in all its forms. Ignoring the wailing girls, he was determined to have his say.

'You god-damned asswipe. You had no call to blast Frank like that. You hear? We've got a right to be in this shithole, same as you. Bodeen's going to bleed you good when he gets back.'

'If he gets back,' snarled Rance, as he moved forward sharply. With all his considerable strength he slammed the shotgun stock into the man's face. He was rewarded with the loud crack of breaking bone, as his victim absorbed the full force of the crushing blow. With his face suddenly unrecognizable, the man tumbled to the floor.

Ignoring the collective wails of the two wounded men, Rance again moved swiftly. He snatched the revolvers from them both and shoved them into his belt. Finally, the town marshal's hard glance took in the remaining revellers. Their party had definitely gone sour and he was about to add to their woes. He had to raise his voice considerably to be heard.

'You skunks lost any right to fair treatment when you accepted fighting wages to invade my town. Those of you who can walk are going to jail.'

Two of those particular men were still fully clothed, but that was about to change.

'You two,' continued Rance. 'Shuck off those pants and boots, then pile all the clothes on the bar.'

Although greeted by disbelief, he

knew exactly what he was about. Bad men without clothes and weapons rapidly lost any air of menace. With Angie watching in wary amusement, both men reluctantly stripped down to their grubby long johns. Their compliance was encouraged by the sight of Frank, the knee-capped regulator, rolling about in great distress. Copious amounts of blood and snot coated the bar room floor.

With the onset of such vicious brutality, Jed had fallen silent. As a saloonkeeper, his speciality was stoking the flames to keep men drinking, whilst personally avoiding any direct involvement. He had witnessed plenty of violence in his time, but all of it from behind the bar. Now he suddenly found himself to be the unwelcome centre of attention.

'Jed,' barked the lawman, 'these two need doctoring. You'd best go fetch him.'

Rance then deliberately allowed the shifty saloonkeeper to get to the main entrance before calling out to him, 'Just one thing: you owe this lady an apology.' Then more ominously, 'Better make it while you can.'

Jed stopped abruptly and half turned. His left eyelid flickered uncontrollably as he searched Rance's face for any indication of humour. There was none. And horrifyingly, the big gun was now pointed unwaveringly at his mid-section. A patina of sweat broke out on his forehead. Real fear assailed him for the first time in many a day, as he realized just what it was like to face up to a genuine killer of men.

'I didn't do nothing to her,' he stammered nervously.

'You didn't show the respect due a lady entering this shithole. Beg her pardon!'

Angie could feel the tension in the air as she watched the clammy barman. With three men standing in their long johns and the moans of the wounded filling the room, she suddenly felt distinctly uncomfortable at the new element of confrontation introduced by the marshal. It was almost as though he enjoyed provoking it. It occurred to her that perhaps Rance wasn't really all that different to the so-called regulators. By pinning on a badge, he had merely legitimized his violent tendencies.

Chewing frantically on his bottom lip, Jed raised his hands in supplication. He genuinely didn't know what he'd done wrong. What he did know was that he was now witnessing a much different side to the Marshal Toller who occasionally had to subdue a rowdy drunk. He carried with him an aura of latent violence that was new and frightening. It made the barkeep realize that the stories of his past exploits in the rough cow towns had to be true.

With his bowels loosening dangerously, Jed cautiously moved towards Angie. Desperately summoning a smile, which in truth was more of a grimace, he looked at her closely for the first time. Despite his trepidation, he couldn't help but think that she was actually quite attractive, which went some way to explaining the marshal's ornery attitude. The bastard obviously had his eye on the prize.

'Apologies if I offended you in any way, ma'am. It was not intended and you're welcome here anytime.'

Jed, realizing that his last remark had tempted providence, eased back towards the door. He hadn't relished being put down, let alone tasting real fear, but perhaps there would be a more favourable time to seek some form of redress. Then again, maybe he was just full of whiskey fumes. Casting a rapid glance at the marshal, he received a taut nod and fled gratefully.

'Weren't you a bit hard on him?' Angie pondered aloud.

'He ain't worth moose piss,' muttered Rance scathingly as he turned back to the others.

The three under-dressed prisoners were a sorry looking bunch as they padded miserably over to the jailhouse. Rance had chivvied them out on to the dark thoroughfare, allowing them plenty of time to take any assassin's bullet before he and Angie had followed. Coming from a brightly lit saloon, the marshal's night vision was non-existent. For this reason alone, he failed to notice the two sorry looking horsemen riding painfully into town.

The state of Angie's eyesight would have been irrelevant anyway, because as the leading prisoner reluctantly opened the jailhouse door she suddenly remembered what they were going to find. All her attention was suddenly focused on that building. As Rance shoved the last one in, a startled voice cried out, 'Jesus Christ, what's that?'

In the gloom, one of the men had collided with the boots of the deceased deputy. Then, as light flared from one of the oil lamps, Clem's poor rigid body was displayed for all to see. His face was pale and wax like. The gaping wound in his throat made it appear as though he possessed another mouth.

Rance swung open the cell door.

'Right boys,' he drawled in a deceptively mild tone. 'Carry my deputy into that cell and place him on the cot.'

The three sad-faced individuals, all of them trembling with cold, stared at their tormentor in amazement. The bravest of them protested, 'We ain't undertakers, mister.'

The lawman swung his shotgun over to cover that man's face. 'You varmints wanted him dead, so now you can watch over his body. Either that or I'll put you in the ground, boy!'

Knowing full well that his words contained no idle threat, all three of them heaved the cadaver out of the swivel chair and into the cell. As soon as they were inside, Rance slammed the heavy iron door and turned the key. Removing it, he then strode outside. By that time the newcomers had moved on, so he missed them again.

When he returned, the key had been replaced in his hand by a small pile of earth and grit from under the boardwalk. Having packed that tightly into the lock, he then grinned brightly at Angie. 'They won't be going anywhere for a while. Come on, let's get out of here.'

She allowed herself to be hustled out of the building, but then halted abruptly and glared up at him defiantly. 'Just what are you about, Rance?' she demanded.

'Things are looking up,' he declared cheerfully. 'I believe that's actually the second time you've called me by my given name and you had a knife at your throat the first time. In case you'd forgotten, we've got a town meeting to attend.'

12

The two bedraggled individuals drifted into town after dark. Frost had formed on their straggly beards. Both men had lost feeling in their extremities. The cold was quite literally deadly. By then neither of them had any interest in killing anyone, which was probably a good thing, because at that moment a group of half-naked men stumbled out of a saloon some way down Main Street. Bizarrely, they appeared to be walking barefoot through the snow. Cole Dekker and the Preacher reined in, just as a tall man carrying a sawn-off shotgun came into view. He was accompanied by a young woman clutching a rifle, who also showed her disdain for the cold by not wearing a coat.

The two frozen horsemen painfully turned in their saddles to exchange bemused glances. Townsfolk were obviously made of stern stuff if they could sashay around undressed on such a night. A startled cry of, 'Jesus Christ, what's that?' drifted over, and then the whole group ended up in the jailhouse with the door closed.

Dekker considered the new development. There was no doubt in his mind that they had just found the marshal, but in their condition and with the actions of their new rifles probably frozen solid, there was not a damn thing they could do about it.

'He'll have to wait,' he mumbled through cracked lips. 'We've got to get under cover.'

Severe lack of funds precluded hotels, saloons or eating-places. Their only choice had to be the livery, wherever that was. There they could doubtless bargain or bully their way under cover. Keeping well wide of the jail, they urged their struggling mounts along the thoroughfare. As luck would have it, they had moved on by the time

Marshal Toller came out of the jail to dispose of the key to the cell door.

The two bone-chilled riders finally ended their journey in front of the livery's large double doors. There was no movement whatsoever on the street. Approaching the smaller inset door, Dekker muttered to his companion, 'I'm not taking sass from any dumb stablehand. We need to get these horses inside. Remember that.'

The Preacher nodded grimly as he pushed against the door. The last poor dumb stablehand to backchat him had ended up slit from crotch to chest. The two remaining scavengers staggered gratefully into the building and looked about.

'Sweet Jesus,' exclaimed the Preacher instinctively.

Six men of varying stature were stood in a line directly facing them. They had to have been expecting someone, but from the expressions on their faces the surprise was mutual.

'Who the hell are you?' demanded

Silas Breckenridge, emboldened by the presence of the other townsfolk.

The two interlopers were dumbfounded, yet resorting to gunplay was not a sensible option. They had no idea who else might be in the vicinity and, of course, their Winchesters were quite likely unusable.

'We're here to meet with Marshal . . . err . . . Toller,' blurted out Dekker. 'We've got a message for him.'

The good citizens of Devil's Lake regarded them dubiously. The two newcomers looked like saddle tramps, pure and simple. On the other hand, if they were there to meet the marshal, then there could be no harm in letting them wait.

'I own these premises,' remarked Silas, always looking to turn a profit. 'You'd best bring your horses in. They'll die on their feet out there.'

So it was that Rance and Angie arrived at the stables to find two strangers leading a pair of played out horses through the main doors. The lawman stopped in his tracks and regarded them carefully. Mind made up, he hissed at Angie, 'Get clear of me!'

The urgency in his voice was plain to hear and she had sense enough to react accordingly. Only when she had disappeared into the shadows did he swing his shotgun over to cover the two men. Cautiously he moved forward, taking care to remain in the gloom.

Years spent evading the law can endow men with certain qualities. The two gunmen somehow sensed movement behind them. Instinctively they released their horses and swung round. This time it was their turn to have no night vision. The marshal was standing just beyond the circle of light spilling out from the livery. All they could clearly see was the double-barrelled crowd tamer pointing vaguely in their direction.

The Preacher was the first with the words. 'Go easy there, friend. We've just come to stable our horses, that's all.'

'Then you won't need those fancy Winchesters,' replied Rance smoothly. 'Dump them!'

Dekker strained to see the features of their hidden assailant. He had no doubt that it was the man that they both sought. He also knew intuitively that they would only get the one chance. Swaying, as though unsteady on his feet, he began talking and at the same time commenced an imperceptible drift to his left. 'We don't just hand our irons over to the first *hombre* who jumps us, mister. You'll have to do better than that.'

At the same time the Preacher also began a gentle shift in position. Silas Breckinridge, having heaved open the doors to his premises, abruptly realized just how uncomfortably close he was to the two men. The situation had suddenly become unaccountably dangerous, but he didn't know what to do for the best.

Rance was not deceived by the fancy footwork. The two men were obviously professionals of a sort, which was all the confirmation that he needed.

'I'm the law in this town and you only get one chance. Let those long irons slide to the ground or get to shooting.'

By way of emphasis, he cocked both the hammers on his big gun.

No longer seeking to protest their innocence, Dekker stopped moving but replied aggressively, 'Better for you if you back right off. There's two of us and only one of you, law dog.'

Completely unfazed, Rance replied blandly, 'You obviously fancy yourself as a shootist, mister. But remember, I've got one barrel for each of you and it's all I'll need.'

It was this uncompromising response that finally unhinged Silas. Due to their furtive movements, he had by now found himself standing just behind and to the side of one of the strangers. If the town marshal opened fire, some of the shot would undoubtedly hit him. Despite the intense cold, beads of sweat broke out on his forehead. The other solid citizens were unarmed and well back inside the building. His stablehand, Thomas, had just simply disappeared. Desperate to get out of the line of fire, Silas moved away from the big door. As he did so his arm caught against the heavy chain used to secure the doors at night.

The metallic jangling triggered a lightning response in the man known as the Preacher. Twisting round, he rapidly worked the under lever and fired. At that range and propelled by seventy-five grains of powder, the bullet caught its victim in his puny chest and literally lifted him off his feet.

Even as Silas's killer began his turn, Rance read the situation and shifted his shotgun directly on to the man who had threatened him. It would not be until much later that regret at the unfortunate turn of events would register with him. Unlike Bodeen, he could not relish the killing of innocent bystanders. For the moment, staying alive was all that concerned him. As his opponent's rifle muzzle swung towards him, he squeezed the first trigger.

Dekker had also heard the chain rattle but, distanced from it, had not felt directly threatened. Expecting the marshal to react to it, he levelled his Winchester. He pushed down on the lever . . . only to discover that it was locked solid. Moisture in the action had frozen hard. That realization was the last thought that he ever had. The awesome blast took him directly in the face, blowing him backwards into the stables. He landed heavily on the hard ground, twitched convulsively a few times and then lay still. With his features just blood and gristle, even his own mother would no longer have recognized him.

The Preacher knew that he was going to meet his Maker even as he pumped up another cartridge. The god-damned marshal knew his trade and would have shifted position in the gloom. It never occurred to him to discard his weapon and plead for mercy. In his time he had killed men, women and children and he intended to go down fighting. He just got off one wild shot before the scattergun crashed out again. The sudden tearing pain was unbelievable. It felt as though all his innards were on fire. Hell had truly claimed him.

Drawing his Remington, Rance cautiously moved into the light. 'Were these the only two?' he called out to the stunned citizenry.

'Ain't you had enough killing, Marshal?' Surprisingly the question came from the dying man before him.

Drawing closer, the lawman kicked the Winchester out of reach. 'Like I said, one barrel for each of you.'

His victim grimaced as fresh blood frothed over his lips. Both men knew that he was mortally wounded. Summoning all his strength, the Preacher managed one last retort. 'You'll need more than that when Bodeen rides in on the morrow.'

He attempted a sardonic laugh but

instead choked on his own juices. His head fell sideways as life gradually drained from his eyes.

Rance swiftly checked Silas for a pulse. He did not expect one and was proved correct. 'Were there any more of them?' he demanded urgently, as he advanced into the building.

Jered Tonks, the portly owner of the only bank in town, observed him warily as he answered. 'Only those two came in here. Can't say how many might be outside. Anyway, how did you know that they'd come for you?'

'Being a marshal ain't just about killing folks, Jered. It's about observation. That's how Bodeen got himself arrested.'

As the banker digested that, Rance reloaded his shotgun before elaborating. 'Those fellows looked like saddle bums. They were underfed and down on their luck, yet they carried the newest and most powerful Winchesters available. It just didn't set right.'

Soft footfalls sounded behind him.

Angie approached, tightly clutching her rifle. Her face was ashen and when she spoke there was an edge of hysteria in her voice. 'When's all this killing going to end?'

Rance favoured her with a gentle smile. He felt truly sorry for the lousy hand that she had been dealt, but there was no easy answer to that. His response also provided the reason for the presence of Devil's Lake's eminent citizens. 'That kind of depends on what these here gentlemen have to say.'

Turning to face the five townsfolk, he looked at each man in turn. All of them appeared deeply uncomfortable and Rance wasn't about to spare their feelings. With Silas destined for a cold hole in the ground, Tonks, the banker, was the most influential man in town, so Rance fixed his eyes on him whilst he spoke. 'You folks appear to have sold this town out from under me. Which, of course, is entirely up to you. Question is, do you still want the law?'

It was plain that all five men wanted

the ground to just swallow them up. None of them could meet his gaze. Finally Jered Tonks managed to string a few words together. 'We never meant for anyone to get hurt, Rance. Bodeen told us that a Chicago syndicate would control the mining. All they wanted was an open town with no one questioning their methods. There'll be fortunes to be made for those who supply their needs. We didn't tell you straight away because you might not have agreed.'

'You're damned right I wouldn't have agreed,' snarled Rance. 'You can't play with the law. You either have it or you don't. When you don't, people get to dying. Mrs Sutter here can testify to that.'

Despite the cold, the banker flushed bright red. 'We never realized Bodeen would kill anyone. He said they just intended to buy out the local home-steaders.'

'Lead's cheaper than gold, Jered. Besides, that man likes killing. It's in his blood. What bothers me is that none of it seems to give you good people pause. So here's what I need to know: do I still carry the law in Devil's Lake or not?'

That question was met with a stunned and embarrassed silence. Rance could hear Angie shuffling behind him, but he ignored her. The matter had to be settled there and then.

Tom Brennen, the mild mannered storekeeper, cleared his throat nervously before finally having his say. 'We knew that you brought a reputation with you, Rance, but we never thought that you'd stand your ground like this.'

So there it was. They had all expected him to run.

The lawman regarded them scornfully as he deliberately stated his case. 'You really don't know what you've got yourselves into. This isn't just some gentlemen's transaction. I've seen men like Bodeen before. He'll promise you the world while you're useful and then gut you like a fish when you're not. As for me, well, I've washed my hands of you all. But not until I've obtained justice for Clem and Mrs Sutter. So when Bodeen and his hired guns ride in tomorrow, I'll be waiting. You good citizens are obviously not with me, so I'll kill any man I see on the street.'

The five good men of Devil's Lake stared at him in stunned amazement. They appeared to have lost any control that they still thought they had over their town. Jered Tonks pulled in his ample gut and attempted to reassert some civic authority.

'We hired you and we can fire you, *Mister* Toller.'

Rance favoured him with a cold smile as he responded, 'Just what are you saying, Jered?'

The danger signs were plain for all to see, but the banker had boxed himself in. He had no choice other than to continue. 'What I'm saying, is that we the citizens' committee need your badge, please.'

As Rance laughed sardonically, he allowed his shotgun to drift upwards. The action did not go unnoticed. Jered paled visibly and, just as with Silas some moment's earlier, beads of sweat suddenly formed on his podgy face.

'You'll get it when I'm through with it,' replied the lawman curtly. 'Come on, Angie, we're all done here.'

As he turned away, he saw something that did surprise him. Standing silently behind the citizens' committee was the stablehand. As their eyes met briefly, that man nodded his head vigorously before retreating back into one of the stalls. Rance had no idea what that signified and was suddenly just too tired to be bothered to pursue him. Without another glance he headed for the hotel, still taking care to take the least visible route. He knew without looking that Angie was following in his wake.

★ ★ ★

Marshal Toller had never got round to either buying or renting a house. On arriving by invitation at Devil's Lake, he had taken a heavily discounted room at the only hotel in town and stayed put. Although he had arranged for a separate room for Angie, she had automatically followed him into his, apparently untroubled by any lack of propriety.

'What the hell was all that about?'

Wearily he looked down at her. It had been a long and brutal day. He really didn't want to answer any more questions.

'I'm dog tired, Angie. Tomorrow's going to blow up like a blue norther so let's just hit the sack.'

'You're going to stay here and take them all on, aren't you? You must have a death wish.'

'Nobody's saying that you have to stay,' he spat back, and then instantly regretted it. 'Listen, not even Bodeen would harm you in town. You can just keep your head down and wait for everything to blow over.'

He might just as well have said nothing for all the notice she took.

'Get that coat off. In case you forgot, you took a bullet earlier. It needs looking at.'

Surrendering to the inevitable, he shrugged out of his clothing. The arm of his linen shirt was covered in dried blood, but underneath the damage was thankfully light. The rifle bullet had merely torn the skin. It was the momentum from the high-powered cartridge that had made it feel like a savage knock.

'You'll live,' she remarked gently as she bathed it with water from his basin. In doing so, her fingers ran lightly over his bare arm. He shivered, although whether that came from the chill in his room or Angie's touch was debatable. With the wound finally clean, she asked for and was given another clean shirt. Tearing a sleeve off, she tied it round his arm.

'You've just ruined a perfectly good shirt,' he remarked flippantly. Then, spontaneously, he leaned down and kissed her lightly on the lips. Despite the raw conditions, they were soft to the touch. He expected her to recoil in shock, but instead she favoured him with a wistful smile.

'It's a little too soon for all that, Rance,' she said softly. 'But I do appreciate your regard.'

With that, she retreated from the room leaving Rance to his thoughts. 'Hot damn,' he considered. 'I ought to get myself shot more often.'

13

The double tap on the door brought him instantly out of a deep sleep. Seizing the Remington from under his pillow, Rance rolled quietly out of bed. Muted daylight showed through the cheap unlined curtains. Positioning himself against the wall next to the entrance, he barked out, 'Who is it?'

A hesitant male voice replied, 'It's me, Marshal — Doyle, from behind the desk.'

Rance sighed regretfully. He had hoped that it might be Angie, coming to return the previous night's kiss.

'Sorry to disturb you,' continued the disembodied voice. 'Only there's some-one to see you.'

Cocking his revolver, the lawman unlocked the door, then backed away and dropped to the floor.

'Send him in,' he commanded. If it

were one of Bodeen's hired killers, he'd consign him straight to the devil!

'He's waiting outside,' came the unhelpful and confusing reply.

It transpired that Rance's mysterious visitor was Thomas, the stablehand. His remaining outside was due to his falling foul of one of the few rules of the establishment, rather than any reluctance to enter on his part. The hotel's owner was a member of the citizens' committee, for which Rance no longer had any regard. Hustling the white-haired individual on to the premises, the marshal sat him down in the lobby and glared pointedly at Doyle. 'Anybody has a problem with this, send them to me,' he remarked.

Under the circumstances, Thomas was nervous but quite obviously determined. 'I heard what you said last night. It ain't right that you have to stand alone against those men. It ain't right at all!'

'Well thank you, Thomas,' replied

Rance, genuinely touched. 'I appreciate the sentiment.'

Presuming that his visitor had come purely as a well-wisher, he rose up ready to usher him out. But there was more to come. Far more.

'Mr Silas didn't just stable horses. He was also a merchant of sorts. Only he dealt in things that no storekeeper would.'

Mystified and suddenly very curious, Rance sat back down. He wondered just where the conversation was leading.

'Right at the back of the livery, under a pile of hay, there are some boxes,' continued Thomas. 'Mr Silas swore me to silence, but that's of no account now. In those boxes there are paper tubes, full of what he called dynamite. He thought to sell it to the gold miners, for blasting and such. Said he was going to make a fortune.'

The lawman gazed at him in wonder. 'That's why the old rogue was always so twitchy.'

Thomas nodded enthusiastically. 'And there was you last night, saying that you'd set the place afire.'

Rance's face creased into a broad smile and he laughed loud and heartily for the first time in many a day. 'If I had, I'd have blown this town all to hell.'

Then, just as suddenly, his lawman's deliberate demeanour returned, as he carefully scrutinized the man. 'Why have you come to tell me this?'

'I know you're in big trouble, Marshal. Lots of bad men are coming here today to kill you. I just thought that you might find a use for some of that contraband.'

Having uttered that evocative word so reminiscent of the days of slavery, he fell temporarily silent. Sensing that there was more to come, Rance wisely held his tongue.

'That Bodeen, he's a Southron. He treated me like I was a piece of no account trash. He fought that war to keep my kind on the plantations, slaves forever. If he and his kind take Devil's Lake, I'll be finished here.' His eyes grew moist as he continued, 'I've lived here quietly and happily for years. I'm too old to have to start again someplace. So you and I have both got reason to stop that evil man, right, Marshal?'

The lawman smiled warmly and patted him on the shoulder. 'Right, Thomas.'

* * *

Sure enough, in an apparently empty stall under an innocuous pile of hay, there turned out to be many boxes of dynamite. Levering the lid off one, Rance tentatively lifted out a small rod of high explosive. It was actually a red paper tube containing a solid stick of nitro-glycerine mixed with an absorbent known as kieselguhr. Unlike the highly unstable nitro-glycerine oil, dynamite could be safely carried. It was vastly more powerful than black powder and was ideal for blasting rock, a fact that Silas would have been fully aware of.

The two men spontaneously exchanged smiles. They both knew only too well that prospecting was the last thing for which the high explosive was now going to be used. Thomas then departed briefly, returning with a burlap sack. Rance counted out a score of dynamite sticks and placed them inside. Getting to his feet, the marshal firmly clasped hands with the stablehand turned conspirator.

'What happened to the fancy Winchesters that those two bull turds arrived with?' he enquired.

'I put them in back, before the undertaker arrived,' replied Thomas slyly. 'That man sees profit in anything.'

The germ of an idea had taken hold in Rance's brain the day before and he was now building on it. 'You keep one of them for yourself, Thomas. It's up to you what you use it for. I want the other one hidden under this hay as a holdout gun. Will you do that for me?'

'Sure will, Marshal. And whatever

you're planning, just make sure that you kill plenty of those southron sons of bitches.'

★　★　★

'I'm right glad I drilled the pus weasel who lived here,' remarked Bodeen with relish. 'This place is a complete shithole. He didn't deserve to live.'

The three cold and weary men had arrived at Barclay's cabin the previous evening. Warmth, shelter and a basic meal had restored their spirits. However, with the arrival of a new day, they discovered just how truly appalling the interior of the dwelling was. The bedding was filthy and there even proved to be a pile of excrement in one corner of the only room. In a warmer climate the smell would have been intolerable.

'He must have done that when he thought you might be outside waiting on him,' commented Seth, wrinkling his nose in distaste. It occurred to him that if Bodeen ever came after him, he'd probably do the same.

'What he needed was a good woman,' announced Charlie Portis, whose thoughts rarely strayed far from that subject.

'We all need one of them,' responded Seth sourly.

Their leader sneered at them disdainfully. He had little tolerance for pointless conversation. 'Enough talk. We're burning daylight. Torch the place!'

His two men were taken aback. 'Why?' queried a puzzled Seth.

'To prove that Marshal Toller ain't the only firestarter in this territory,' snarled Bodeen with an emphatic air of finality. 'Get it done!'

* * *

Hefting the heavy sack in his left hand, Rance eased open the livery door. He carefully surveyed the frozen thoroughfare. Not a living thing was in sight. As far as he could make out, not one business had opened up. Devil's Lake resembled a played-out ghost town, rather than a relatively prosperous community.

'What day is it, Thomas?'

That man pondered for a moment and then smiled widely. 'In all the excitement I'd just plain forgotten. It's Christmas Eve, Marshal.'

'Let's see if we can't celebrate with a few fire crackers. Whatever happens, don't come anywhere near the hotel. You hear?' With that, Rance slipped out of the building and retraced his steps. There was one other person he had to see before he set to work.

* * *

Angie greeted the contents of the sack with total disbelief. 'Do you know how to use those things?'

'I know how to light a fuse,' replied Rance testily. 'I'll learn the rest as I go along.' Even as he uttered that, it occurred to him that he was being frighteningly optimistic, but like most men he was unwilling to admit lack of knowledge on any subject.

'What if some of the buildings are damaged?' she persisted.

'The good citizens should have thought of that before taking up with a gang of murderers and cutthroats. For me, I don't really care anymore. Once I've finished here, I'm leaving along with anyone who might choose to come along.'

Now that did give her pause. She stared at him long and hard, as though trying to gauge his true meaning. Finally she reached over and took his hand.

'I haven't quite decided what sort of man you are yet. There's times you make me downright nervous. But I guess we'll have to give it some time.'

Rance's heart leapt with joy, until the grim realization of what had to be done first brought him back to earth. She saw his expression and knew just what it meant.

'What's going to happen here?' she asked earnestly.

The lawman had been doing a lot of thinking and welcomed the chance to put his plans into words. They were in her room, again ignoring any improprieties, so he sank down onto her bed and began talking. 'Bodeen will doubtless have spent last night in Barclay's cabin. He could be here anytime soon, but I believe he will endeavour to meet up with his reinforcements before coming into town. He underestimated me before, he won't make that mistake again. He most likely doesn't know what's happened to his two assassins, or even what his own men might be up to.'

Angie watched him closely as he spoke. There was a cold practicality to him that was almost chilling. Yet, she reminded herself, without such qualities they would have little chance of survival. She was under no illusions about her own chances without Rance. Bodeen was unlikely to let her live after what had taken place.

'He won't be overly confident of his numbers this time,' he continued, oblivious of her critical scrutiny. 'He'll split his force and come in, on foot, from both ends of town. He may check Pearsall's first, but one way or another he'll end up at the jailhouse. That's where *we'll* catch him.'

She hadn't missed the emphasis on that word. So he'd known all along that she wouldn't stay out of it.

'We do have one thing Bodeen could never expect: artillery!' With that, he smiled and got up. 'You go get some food, while I go down to the jailhouse. There's something I need to get.'

'There you go giving me orders again,' Angie replied lightly. But she went anyway.

★ ★ ★

'You poxy son of a bitch,' bawled one of the prisoners. 'We'll likely freeze to death in here if you don't let us out.'

The others joined in with similar protests, which Rance completely ignored. Approaching the gun rack, he removed the only remaining weapon. The previous year an inebriated salesman of dubious elixirs had reluctantly surrendered a Spencer carbine. After sobering up, curiously he had left town without reclaiming it. Embarrassment sometimes took people that way. Although the early repeater was a bit of an antique, its .50 calibre bullet was definitely a man-stopper and had been popular with the Union forces. The marshal had developed a bit of a soft spot for it, so much so that he had taken to occasionally oiling and polishing it. The carbine boasted a full tubular magazine and would serve as another weapon of last resort.

Pausing momentarily at the door, the lawman blandly remarked, 'Sorry, boys, I've gone and mislaid the only key.' With that, he headed across the street to Pearsall's Emporium.

Devil's Lake was a relatively compact town. At one end of the main thoroughfare, the jailhouse faced the hotel. The main building of note at the other end was the livery. Pearsall's was next to the hotel, allowing the two to feed off each other's custom. Various timber houses belonging to the permanent residents were to be found bordering three smaller side streets.

Rance smiled grimly as he strode into the saloon. It occurred to him that not all the structures might survive that day. The gaudy premises were completely deserted. It took a lot to stop some men drinking even at that early hour, but the fear of violent death had obviously had that effect. Entering the familiar storeroom, he tucked the heavy carbine behind some wooden packing cases and then retraced his steps. The marshal would perhaps have felt a touch uneasy, had he only known that his progress had been observed.

*   *   *

The two groups of heavily armed riders cautiously approached each other on the Grand Forks road, north east of the town. Three men came in from the west, whilst the other fifteen were new arrivals in the area. Their clothing and backgrounds were varied, but they all bore the same mark: the edgy, hunted look of the hired gun.

There followed a lengthy exchange of words, as Dan Bodeen explained the situation. Then they were all on the move again, but very slowly and carefully. Two men fanned out ahead of the main body. This time there would be no mistakes.

* * *

As Angie watched Rance Toller enter her room, she felt a vague unease. For a man soon to confront a gang of hired killers, he looked too composed. It was almost as though he relished the prospect, whereas she was quite frankly terrified of the likely consequences. Then he favoured her with a broad smile and her doubts faded. But for him, she would have died at the hands of the consumptive road agent. The marshal was the only man in town prepared to make a stand against big business and its thugs. He was also overloaded, with a Winchester and shotgun cradled in his left arm and the burlap sack in his right hand.

'This is your last chance to get clear of me,' he stated earnestly.

'No. I made a vow to avenge Jacob,' she replied firmly, and then added with a bright smile, 'Anyhow, you know you can't do this without me.'

He gave her a long smouldering look, as though he had more than just hired guns on his mind. Then the moment passed and it was down to business of a different kind.

'Get your coat on. We're going on the roof. I need you to carry this shotgun for me.'

Bristling with weapons, they left her first-floor room. As they moved along the corridor, a bedroom door opened abruptly. A florid, middle-aged gentleman carrying a large carpetbag viewed them severely. He appeared on the point of venturing a comment, but obviously thought better of it. Touching his hat in deference to her sex, the man hurriedly departed.

'Looks like he had business elsewhere,' remarked Rance drily.

At the end of the corridor they found a trapdoor leading onto the roof. A solid wooden ladder was connected by a hinge to a joist on the ceiling, with its bottom step secured by a tie rope to a metal bracket. Leaping up, Rance swiftly released this and the ladder swung down ready for use. Swarming up it, he heaved the trapdoor out of the way and so clambered out onto the roof.

Burdened by the shotgun and her own Henry rifle, Angie followed awkwardly. The air that awaited her held a biting chill. Crouching down, Rance crept over to the low parapet. Peering over cautiously, he made a long and intensive study of the townscape. He saw a community held in the vicelike grip of winter. Smoke plumed from every chimney, confirming the fact that everybody was wisely staying off the streets. It was dull and overcast. The light was quite probably as good as it was going to get. As yet there was no sign of Bodeen's illegitimate posse. Finally satisfied, the marshal turned to his deputy.

'There is a Spencer carbine hidden in the storeroom at Pearsall's and a new-fangled Winchester over at the livery.' As he spoke, his eyes grew hard and cold. 'Remember, if they should get past me, their blood will be up. They won't take any prisoners, so keep shooting until they're dead or you run out of bullets!'

* * *

Planning his strategy on the ride in had enabled Dan Bodeen to temporarily forget the bone chilling cold. As the rooftops showed through the frost glazed trees, he reined the column in and divided his forces. Half were to sweep round the town, dismount and then carefully approach the jail on foot. He and the remaining eight would come in near the livery, also on foot. He had no idea whether his two pitiful assassins had struck pay dirt, or even if his own men had got the drop on Toller. If they hadn't, then it was his hunch that any gunplay would start near the jailhouse, and he would be on hand to observe the fall of shot. One way or another, this time Marshal Rance Toller was definitely a dead man!

* * *

Rance was carefully trimming the fuses on a selection of dynamite sticks when he sensed rather than heard movement. The existing fuses were timed for blasting inert rock rather than alert human beings. Angie was further along the roof, watching the livery. To his eyes, she looked small and vulnerable but there was no longer any time for sentiment.

Bringing his eyes level with the parapet, he scanned the town limits. Nine men with weapons raised were cautiously approaching the town. All were heavily muffled against the cold, but their gun hands were uncovered. They were spread out in a wide arc so as to avoid the dangers of bunching up. Bodeen did not appear to be amongst them, which likely meant there were more coming in from the other end.

Turning away, Rance found Angie frantically signalling. She raised all the fingers of both hands. Even if she had over estimated, it still meant that they had suddenly got an awful lot to handle. Giving her a curt nod by way of acknowledgement, he retrieved a box of lucifers from an inner pocket. His Winchester, cocked and ready, was leaning against the parapet. It had begun!

14

Nine men, who made their living by bullying, threatening and very occasionally killing someone, were spread in a wide semi-circle around the front of the jailhouse. They were all professionals of a sort and had been graphically forewarned about the man that they were hunting. Four of them faced the jail, whilst the remainder covered the surrounding buildings. Tense and unseasonably clammy, they thought that they were ready for anything. Yet, although hardened to their way of life, none of them could have anticipated the sheer immensity of the assault that was about to be unleashed.

* * *

Up behind the parapet, Angie remained at her post with firm instructions to hold her fire until their position was discovered. A lucifer flared into life. Rance had never handled explosives before and he was about to get a very sharp lesson in their use. In his right hand, he clutched two of the red-coloured sticks. As the naked flame touched the fuses, both burst into vivid life.

Christ, they're burning fast, was his only thought as he frantically tossed them over the side. One exploded in the slush, whilst the other airburst some-where between the hotel and jailhouse. The concussion from the terrific explosions took his breath away. Earth and mucky water showered over him and then the screaming started.

* * *

Down by the livery, Bodeen cautiously advanced at the centre of his eight widely spaced cronies. The other group was clearly visible at the far end of town, apparently ready for any possible danger. The twin detonations seemed to come from nowhere. The windows on either side of those men shattered. Earth and slush flew into the air. Instinctively, he and the men around him dropped to the ground. With their faces in the dirt, they heard rather than witnessed the next brace of explosions.

'Sweet Jesus,' bellowed Bodeen. 'Where are they coming from?'

* * *

Rance had no idea what effect his missiles were having. His good ear was ringing painfully from the blasts, but he kept his head down and lit two more anyway. This time he threw them into the street vigorously, so that they both went off at ground level. Two more massive explosions reached up to him, temporarily drowning out the screams. Risking a quick look at Angie, he saw that she was still crouching down, which suggested that Bodeen's group had gone to ground. He decided to use two more sticks and then take a look-see. Striking another lucifer, Rance got the fuses hissing, stood up and threw the dynamite further over towards the jail. He could only imagine the chaos and panic amongst the prisoners securely penned in that small cell.

* * *

Bodeen's men had their faces firmly in the slush, but not him. Desperately seeking the source of the explosions, he happened to be looking directly at the hotel, just as the lawman overplayed his hand by briefly showing himself.

'The bastard's on the hotel roof,' hollered Bodeen, as two more detonations rang out. 'You're not paid to lie around. Get shooting!'

His words galvanized his men into action. Their powerful rifles spat out a rapid fire, so that chunks of wood flew off the parapet at the far end of the building. It suddenly occurred to him that Toller might not be alone up there.

Leaping to his feet, he ran for the boardwalk. His men, belatedly realizing their vulnerability, followed suit.

* * *

Angie had never before in her life heard noise like it. The massive explosions and subsequent screaming was absolutely terrifying. She just wanted to curl up in a ball and hide. But then bullets began to hit the woodwork at the far end of the roof. The thought that Rance might need help overcame her fear. Cocking her rifle, she risked a quick look down the street. Over by the livery, Dan Bodeen clambered to his feet and ran to cover. By the time his men sought to do the same, she was ready. Lining up on a likely target, Angie squeezed the trigger. Without waiting to see the result, she worked the under lever and fired again and again.

* * *

Bodeen's group suddenly found itself under accurate and deadly fire. One man took a snub-nosed bullet in the throat. He tumbled to the ground in a welter of blood never to rise again. Next, Charlie Portis took a bullet in his left shoulder. It spun him around, leaving him dazed and befuddled. His life was saved by an unknown companion pulling him over to the telegraph office.

'God damn it to hell,' snarled Bodeen. 'How many's he got up there?' Viewing his remaining men with disdain, he barked out, 'Keep off the street and follow me. We've got to stop that law dog before he leaves the hotel and goes to ground someplace else.'

Keeping close to the buildings, they all moved along the boardwalk. There was more gunfire, but none of it seemed to be coming their way.

★ ★ ★

Rance heard the reassuring bark of Angie's Henry further along the roof.

Recovering his own carbine, he risked a look over the parapet. He had expected the slush to be covered with mutilated men and severed body parts, replicating the worst days of the War Between the States. It had not occurred to him that explosives needed to be surrounded by other material to do the maximum damage. Nevertheless, at such close range, blast and concussion had served him well. Four men lay sprawled about, bleeding profusely from their ears and noses. Another had been badly sliced up by flying glass and was completely out of the fight. It was that unfortunate who had done most of the screaming. The remaining gunmen had escaped serious harm and were scurrying for shelter. Disorientated by the explosions, none of them knew where the attack had come from. Two ran for the hotel whilst the others made for the jail. Swiftly lining up on one of the latter, Rance squeezed off a shot. The bullet caught his victim squarely between the shoulder blades, throwing him forward

213

into the already shattered window. Rapidly pumping the under lever, he aimed and fired again. The gun thug must have said his prayers that day, because just at that moment he stumbled on the sidewalk planking and the shot went wide. Rance cursed and levered in another cartridge, but by then the tables had turned. His intended victim was inside the jail and returning fire.

Ducking down, the marshal considered his options. If left to his own devices, that lone gunman would probably end up freeing his *compadres* in the cell. Casting a glance at Angie, he saw that she was unhurt and reloading her repeater. 'Where's Bodeen?' he hissed.

Jumping slightly, as though shocked out of her own little world, she replied, 'They're moving up towards us under cover. I can't get a shot.'

Mind made up, Rance called back, 'Get over to the trap door with the shotgun and keep watch.'

Obeying without question, his deputy scurried over to the hatch. Placing her rifle on the roof, she cocked both hammers of the shotgun and crouched down in readiness.

Rance meanwhile selected two sticks of dynamite with undoctored fuses and struck another match. As the explosives flared into life, he stepped well back from the parapet and rose to his full height. Concealed from anyone below, he took aim at the jailhouse and hurled them with all his might. Hissing and twisting in the air, the deadly missiles flew unerringly on to the roof.

* * *

Bodeen led his men along the side of the main street without attracting any more flying lead. He had seen two survivors of the explosions head into Pearsall's and intended to meet them there. Those men still lying in the street in great distress would just have to wait; he had more pressing business. Just as he reached the dry goods store, two flying objects registered on his peripheral vision.

'Hit the dirt!' he yelled out, and did just that.

For long seconds nothing happened. The regulators' leader was just reflecting that he had possibly over-reacted, when suddenly there were two almost simultaneous explosions on the roof of the jailhouse. The whole timber structure collapsed in on itself. Dust and chunks of wood flew everywhere. Fresh screaming emanated from the ruined structure. The horrendous injuries likely sustained from wood splinters didn't bear thinking about, so he didn't.

'Get off the deck and into the hotel,' Bodeen commanded. 'The tarnal son of a bitch won't want to blow himself up.'

As the men pounded past the saloon, he hollered at the two survivors to follow on. Half of his men were effectively out of the fight and he hadn't even had Toller in his sights once. Rage was boiling within him. That marshal was going to die, even if they had to destroy the whole town to achieve it.

* * *

Rance viewed the wrecked jail with genuine remorse, not because of the casualties within it — they had brought such retribution on themselves — but that building had been his place of work for some good years and now it had all gone. As if confirming this fact, smoke began to drift up from the ruin. The contents of a shattered oil lamp must have ignited in the explosion. It appeared as though Clem was to be laid to rest by cremation rather than burial, along with the other unfortunates in the cell. Renewed screaming validated the fact that they weren't all dead. At least one of Bodeen's thugs faced a truly horrendous demise.

Because his attention was so strongly held by the grim scene, it was some time before other movement beyond that building registered with him.

Alarm and puzzlement seized him with equal measure as he peered over at the new development. People were advancing out into the virgin snow. Lots of people, large and small, young and old. They were riding horseback, on wagons and in buggies. The whole population of Devil's Lake was getting safely out of range of the war that had abruptly broken out in their town. As if to emphasize the soundness of their decision, the crash of a shotgun came from behind him. Twisting around, he saw powdersmoke drifting away from Angie's weapon.

'The devils are in the corridor, Rance.'

* * *

Bodeen cursed fluently as he was showered with plaster and woodchips. The shotgun had discharged the very second that they had reached the top of the stairs. Moving back down behind his men, he yelled out, 'Let's rush them, boys. There can't be but two of them up there.'

The hired guns shuffled about, but made no move to comply. All of them knew that they weren't up against some tenderfoot, who would just scare at the first rush.

'God-damned pansies,' snarled their leader as he stormed back down to the deserted lobby. His powerful form barrelled over to the main entrance. He was met by a penetrating scream emanating from the flaming jailhouse. It was accompanied by the sickly sweet stench of burning flesh. He was in no all-fired hurry to venture on to the street, but thankfully he suddenly discovered that he didn't need to. One of those men stunned by the first explosions had somehow got to his feet and stumbled to the nearest shelter. Blood trickled from his nose and ears. He was staring wild-eyed into the middle distance. It was quite obvious that he was in severe shock.

Grabbing him by the collar, Bodeen

frog-marched him into the hotel. The man mumbled unintelligible protests and vainly tried to struggle free. Swiftly drawing his Colt, his supposed leader rammed it hard into his ribs. 'Get up those stairs, asswipe, or I'll shoot you myself.' Then to the others, he called out, 'Make way there, god damn it!'

Those men huddled at the top of the stairs looked on askance at the treatment of one of their own. A tall, hard-faced character, with what looked like a duelling scar on his left cheek, even had the temerity to protest. 'Hey there, Dan. You ain't got no call to treat him like that. He ain't himself yet.'

Bodeen sprang at him like a striking snake. His vitriol came hard and fast and seemed strangely jumbled. 'Then he shouldn't have got himself blown up. That marshal is cutting us down like ripe wheat. He and his whore are up there laughing at me. No one gets the drop on Dan Bodeen. No one!'

Far from backing off, the other man merely sneered, 'The way I heard it,

Toller did that and more. Even locked you in a cell.'

The gunshot was so unexpected that even the gang of hardened cutthroats flinched. Powder flash-induced smoke blossomed from the man's coat. He peered down at it in stunned amazement, before giving a strangled cry. Blood pumped out of the ghastly wound and splashed over his boots. As all feeling left his body, he fell heavily against the banister, which promptly collapsed under his weight.

Dismayed at their companion's sudden death, the other men backed down the stairs. Bodeen swung round to cover them with his still smoking Colt. His brutalized features were contorted with rage. So distracted was he that he failed to react to the sound of rending wood and metal that came from the trapdoor. Instead, he stated his case to the watching gunnies.

'I aim to kill me that marshal and his bitch. You're either with me or agin me. Anybody else want to *drop* out?'

The group clustered on the stairs regarded him warily. They were all hardened to violence, but Dan Bodeen was in a different league. He was an unhinged mad dog, who, unfortunately, just happened to pay their wages. Taking their silence as acquiescence, Bodeen turned back towards the hotel corridor. The injured man who had inadvertently sparked the gunplay was sitting on the stairs, oblivious to the turmoil. As it turned out, he was no longer needed.

* * *

The single gunshot was clearly audible up on the roof.

'Looks like they're having a little disagreement,' Rance remarked lightly. Joining Angie at the trapdoor, he added, 'If they're starting to kill each other, we might get out of this yet. Cover me with that scattergun.'

Getting down on to his knees, the

lawman used the butt of his Winchester to smash at the hinge securing the ladder to the ceiling below them. It soon crumbled under the violent impact, enabling him to drag the wooden steps up onto the roof.

'What are you about, Rance?' queried Angie curiously.

'We were never going to come down off this roof through the hotel: there's too many guns down there. Likewise, Bodeen's not coming up. So, we're back to the usual choices: wait us out or burn us out. That skunk hasn't got the patience to just sit around.'

Her eyes flitted over to the burlap bag. He laughed and shook his head. 'Using that down there would like as not blow us both to kingdom come. No, our best bet is to just let him do what he's going to do.'

*　*　*

Bodeen acknowledged the lack of a roof ladder by calling back to his men. 'Get me some oil lamps up here, burning bright.'

They duly arrived, their wicks adjusted to provide a vivid flame. As though in recognition of the threat, a shotgun blast came from the trapdoor. Its deadly projectiles peppered the corridor, but no one was hurt.

'Heave them at the walls, boys,' commanded Bodeen.

As the lamps smashed, burning oil flared up the papered walls, rapidly turning the corridor into a blazing inferno.

'That marshal likes to play with fire,' remarked Seth gleefully, having witnessed the barn fire at first hand. 'Let's see him get out of this one, hey.'

★ ★ ★

The regulator might not have been so smug, if he could have seen what 'that marshal' was about. Having anticipated the new turn of events, Rance had carried the stepladder to the rear of the hotel. Lining it up with Pearsall's Emporium, he nodded to Angie and simply let go. As the shotgun crashed out, the ladder slammed down on to Pearsall's roof. Its length was only just sufficient to cover the gap between the two buildings.

Rance shivered as he regarded the drop. Although only two floors, it still looked an awfully long way down. Heights of any kind had always made him nervous and the open spaces between the individual steps left little to the imagination. Angie joined him at the edge, weighed down with weapons and the remaining dynamite. The sight of the burlap sack gave him an idea. Removing three sticks, he returned swiftly to the trapdoor. Down below, flames were taking hold on the woodwork. They would inevitably be drawn upwards by the fresh air. Rance placed the explosives near the opening and hurried back to his companion.

They had to move fast. Bodeen's men would only remain in the hotel until they were sure that he could not drop down through the hatch. After that they would most likely spill outside to prevent any escape. He was heartened to see that Angie was already on the ladder. With her Henry in one hand and his empty shotgun in the other, she was moving steadily and without any apparent fear from rung to rung. Safely across on the roof of the saloon, she turned to him with a triumphant smile.

God, she's attractive, he thought, not for the first time, before his own particular predicament returned to haunt him. The gap appeared a lot wider than it had before. Signalling for her to catch the bag of dynamite, he threw it over to her. Deftly catching it, she then waited for him to join her.

Gripping his Winchester far more tightly than was necessary, Rance gingerly stepped on the first rung. He knew that he had to be quick, before either the dynamite blew or he was spotted. Yet that knowledge only seemed to make things worse. As he looked down, the ground seemed to drift closer and then retreat. He felt strangely light-headed. Maybe it was the burst eardrum that was affecting him. As sweat began to form on his brow, he forced himself to advance. First one rung, then another and then the ladder seemed to tremble. He froze in terror. What if it couldn't take his weight?

'Rance, what's wrong?' Angie's voice was low and urgent.

Seemingly rooted to the spot, he couldn't even answer her. Every fibre of his being was concentrated on just staying aloft. She obviously realized his predicament, because she next attempted to give advice.

'Rance, whatever you do, don't look down. Look at me instead. Look straight at me, Rance!'

At that moment there was movement below him. Two of Bodeen's hired guns came around the front of the hotel and down the alley. They were there to watch the roof, which is exactly what they did. The one in front looked up and saw the marshal looming above him, immobile on the ladder. The man's eyes widened in surprise. 'Tarnation, it's him,' he called to his companion, as he raised his rifle.

15

The shock of discovery overcame Rance's dread of heights. Swinging his carbine down, he took rapid aim and fired. The bullet took the leading gun hand in his chest. The momentum threw him back at his companion just as that man also fired. The bullet flew high and wide, but did succeed in stirring Rance into action. Choosing movement over gunplay, he advanced on the ladder.

The man below him levered in another cartridge and tried again. With a tremendous crack the projectile struck the side of the wooden ladder. Panic-stricken, the lawman released his carbine and dropped to his knees. They jarred painfully against a rung at the same instant as his Winchester landed in the slush. Cursing fluently, the gunman again pumped the action of his repeater. In the heat of the moment it never occurred to him to check the rooftops.

Angie drew a careful bead and squeezed the trigger. Her aim was true and, as the second man crumpled to the ground, she hollered out, 'You hear me, Rance Toller? Stop this tomfoolery and get over here now!'

His eyes met hers across the void. 'Yes, ma'am,' he replied, getting to his feet. Spread-eagling his arms like Christ on the cross, he placed his trust in her and began walking. Within seconds he was on Pearsall's roof, feeling decidedly foolish but not a little relieved.

'What was all that about?' she enquired curiously. She appeared little troubled at having just killed another human being. The brutalizing effect of combat was already beginning to show.

'I'll tell you later,' he replied as he shoved the ladder clear of the roof. Even as it fell to the ground, he realized his mistake. They could possibly have used it again in some way. Shaking his head in dismay, he continued, 'We need to find a way down and fast.'

★ ★ ★

In the hotel lobby, Bodeen heard the rapid exchange of gunfire as he watched the flames billowing down the stairs. 'Get out there,' he bawled, at the dwindling band of men around him. Dutifully, they raced outside and spread out along the boardwalk, keeping clear of the open street. They were all acutely mindful of their opponents' lethal ability with any weapon that came to hand. As their leader arrived at the end of the alley, he took in the ladder and the two dead men and groaned.

'Any man who brings me the head of this son of a bitch gets a five hundred dollar bounty!'

That generous offer was greeted by a monstrous explosion on the hotel roof. Blazing timber rained down around them, followed by a cloud of ash. Glancing around fearfully, the gunmen retreated down the street, past the saloon and on to the dry goods store. For some time they milled around in confusion, wondering just what might happen next.

'That cockchafer's blowing this town all to hell,' remarked one of them apprehensively. Even as he spoke, there was a roar as the far wall of the hotel fell in to the building. The whole structure had become a raging inferno, which was quite capable of spreading to Pearsall's Emporium.

Recovering from the shock of the blast before his men, Bodeen recalled the position of the ladder and suddenly knew exactly where his prey was. 'They're in Pearsall's' piss pit. Get in there now!'

★   ★   ★

Rance and Angie were in a corridor on the first floor of the saloon when the dynamite detonated. They had discovered a trapdoor on the roof, which had allowed them access to the building. The timber structure seemed to tremble under the shock of the violent explosion. Instinctively, Angie gripped his arm for reassurance, which was somewhat laughable, as he had caused the devastation in the first place. He welcomed the intimacy, but something else had also taken his attention. From beyond one of the doors he had just heard a heavy footfall. If all the town's citizens had fled, then anyone remaining had to be a potential threat.

Rance cocked his reloaded shotgun and, without hesitation, kicked in the flimsy barrier. To his surprise the curtains were drawn against the weak December light, so that the room was not only cold but dark as well. That did not prevent him spotting the small shape huddled near the bed.

'Show yourself,' he demanded. His big gun was aimed unwaveringly at the figure as it slowly moved towards him. For some reason he shivered involuntarily, prompted by a strange uneasiness.

Although a shawl concealed the features, from the size it had to be either a woman or child. The figure halted directly in front of him, face tilted downwards. Something stopped him from reaching out with his left hand. Instead he used the gun muzzles to remove the wrap.

As it slid away, the light from the corridor shone on the wreckage that had once been her face. Angie had also entered the room, and she gasped with horror at what she saw. The woman's features were literally covered in watering lesions and pustules. Such was the extent of the damage that it was impossible to guess at her age or even discern whether she might once have been pretty. Angie took a step back. If the creature had wet leprosy she wanted no contact whatsoever.

It was Rance who realized the true reason for the female's appalling condition. He had seen ill-used prostitutes before, but never one with her level of decay. 'Those are syphilitic sores,' he explained softly. 'This little lady's been a working girl. Haven't you?'

The woman looked up and her surprisingly clear blue eyes met his. She nodded once and then flinched as a tremendous crash came from the direction of the hotel. Rance placed his left hand gently on her shoulder as he spoke. 'We *all* need to get out of here. That fire's going to spread and this place is next in line.'

That small token of human contact suddenly opened the floodgates. 'Jed won't be right pleased if I go downstairs. He only lets me stay here so long as no one sees me. Says it's for my own good.' She paused and then added by way of explanation, 'I used to be his girl.'

The lawman snorted. His reply was laced with sarcasm. 'Well he's certainly done right by you.'

From below there came the sound of heavy footsteps and harsh male voices. Glancing meaningfully at Angie, he addressed an urgent question to the woman. 'Is there a back way out of here?'

Her reply was swift and assured. 'There's some narrow stairs that come out near the storeroom. They come in useful in a whorehouse,' she added helpfully.

'I can imagine,' replied Angie drily.

'Show us now,' cut in Rance, who had heard a footfall on the main stairs.

Mind apparently made up, the woman swiftly led them back along the corridor, then through a narrow archway. Sure enough a set of very steep stairs led directly down to the storeroom. They were concealed by a grubby curtain, which explained why he had not noticed them before.

'There's something I need to get,' he whispered, before heading over to the wooden packing cases. The Spencer carbine that he had concealed earlier would serve as a useful replacement for his Winchester except that it was no longer where he had placed it!

'God damn it,' he snarled bitterly.

He had barely uttered the words when the door from the saloon opened and two men entered the room. They were ready for trouble. Their rifles were raised and they knew their trade, but they had just stepped from a brightly lit room into a darkened one. They had unwittingly lost their edge and it cost them dearly.

Swinging his shotgun around, Rance fired once, then again. There were two massive discharges and the men were literally blasted back into the gaudy saloon. Only one of them managed to get a shot off, but the result was not immediately apparent. Then the real bloodletting began.

From behind the curtain that they had just come through, a fusillade of shots ripped out. Something viciously hot tore at Rance's left side. The shocking pain seemed to trigger a fighting madness that coursed through his veins. Hurling the empty shotgun at the curtain, he swiftly drew his Remington. Screaming at Angie to cover the door, he cocked and fired four times. As the revolver bucked in his hand, sulphurous smoke filled the room. From the hidden stairs, a high-pitched scream erupted. Then Angie's Henry crashed out once. More firing came from the saloon and an agonizing pain lanced into his right leg. Stumbling under the impact, he fell heavily onto a table.

Angie spotted his predicament with her peripheral vision and screamed out 'Rance', but she still had the sense to keep on firing. Concealed by the smoky blackness, she levered and fired, levered and fired. Such a weapon had been enough to put hardened rebels to flight in the late conflict, and Angie Sutter was like a woman possessed.

Although engulfed by pain, the marshal knew that he could not give in to it. The burlap sack with the last of his dynamite was conveniently on the floor beneath him. Sliding off the table, he dropped to his knees next to it. Sheer agony snaked across his injured right leg. His side was greasy with blood and he could feel vomit rising in his throat.

More shots rang out in the saloon. Their situation was truly desperate.

Working by touch, he removed a stick with a short fuse. Then, reaching into his jacket pocket, he pulled out his remaining lucifers. Somehow he managed to strike one, although the rest fell out of his shaking hands, lost forever. Holding the naked flame to the fuse, he yelled at Angie to take cover and then tossed the hissing explosive into the saloon. With an ear splitting roar the solid nitro-glycerine detonated.

★ ★ ★

Dan Bodeen was creeping along the first-floor corridor when the shooting broke out. For once in his brutal life he was unsure how to proceed. He knew about the back stairs, as did anyone with a taste for whores. He had just sent one of his men to check them out. As the shooting intensified, an agonized scream came from the bottom of the stairwell and he abruptly decided to try his luck at the front. Pounding down the main stairs, rifle at the ready, he was met with a concussive blast that threw him bodily off his feet. There was a roaring in his ears and sharp objects seemed to be slicing into his face. Rolling over, he desperately shook his head and very slowly the noise seemed to recede.

Bodeen had no idea how long he lay there. As his vision returned, he could see blood pooling on the floor in front of his face. He knew that he was hurt, but not where. Then the numbness wore off and suddenly suffering engulfed him. Staggering weakly to his feet, the regulators' leader gazed around at the carnage in the room. It was then that it occurred to him that he quite possibly wasn't the leader of anything any more.

Five of his men lay dead, although how they had died wasn't clear. Every window and every mirror in the place was shattered. By chance a single fragment of the large mirror behind the bar remained in its frame. Drifting over to it, he peered at his reflection. His features were scorched, grimy and almost unrecognizable. Blood seeped out of numerous cuts. His eyebrows had completely gone. Suddenly aware that he no longer held his Sharps, Bodeen drew his revolver and frenziedly smashed the glass into tiny pieces.

Mouthing vague obscenities, he finally turned away to recover his rifle. The door to the storeroom was wide open. The law dog and his bitch could only have left through there. As Bodeen cautiously entered the room, he saw a small and quite obviously feminine figure lying face down. Joy surged through what passed for his heart, as he realized that Sutter's widow had finally met her death. Closing in for a better look, he eased his boot under her slight body and heaved her over.

'What the hell's that?' His response was entirely involuntary. The single bullet that had killed her had struck her lower jaw, entirely shattering it. As a consequence she was disfigured, but not half as much as she had been before the gunfight.

'Jesus, what a mess,' he muttered. Then, as it dawned on his befuddled brain that the woman could not possibly be Angie Sutter, he turned on his heels and charged back through the saloon. Bursting out through the main entrance, the blood-soaked gunman stopped abruptly. The wall of heat that struck him was almost overwhelming. The jailhouse was just a smoking ruin, whereas the much larger hotel had become a raging fire storm. It could not be long before the saloon was also engulfed. Bizarrely, the snow in that section of town had completely melted. A once frozen thoroughfare had swiftly turned into a sea of mud.

Retreating before the fire, Bodeen desperately searched the street for any signs of life. Surely all seventeen of his men couldn't have been slain? Then he saw them. Two of the dazed survivors of the first ambuscade were lying on the boardwalk in front of the milliner's store, two buildings in from the jail. To get to them meant crossing the killing ground of the open street, but he really had little choice. He needed men and they were displaying no inclination to move.

Gathering himself, he sucked in a deep breath and ran like hell. The expected gunfire did not materialize and the two men soon found their leader looming over them, his Sharps rifle hovering in their general direction. Bodeen had no idea of their names and he didn't give a damn. They looked muddy, bloodstained and beaten, but at least they were alive — which would answer, because all he needed was bait.

'Get on your feet, god damn it. We've got a job to finish.'

The two regulators regarded him with sullen disbelief. They were sorely tempted to ignore him, but then the ominous click of a rifle hammer brought them back to a highly unpleasant reality. Clambering reluctantly to their feet, one of them made a token protest. 'We ain't ourselves yet, Mr Bodeen.'

Thrusting his charred and bloody features towards them, that man snarled, 'Do I look like I care?'

* * *

Having left Pearsall's by the rear door, the two fugitives had paralleled the main street until they came level with the livery. Their progress was necessarily slow. Rance was favouring a leg wound, whilst Angie had to both support him and carry her rifle and the few remaining sticks of dynamite. She had been all for leaving those to the encroaching flames, but he wouldn't run the risk of Bodeen getting his hands on them.

As they approached the livery, the door was unexpectedly opened from the inside. They were greeted by a rifle muzzle, followed by a smiling face.

'Holy mother of God,' exclaimed Rance. 'I don't know what kept you here, but I'm powerful glad to see you, Thomas.'

The other man replied with what had to be the understatement of the century. 'I heard a noise!' With that, he chuckled softly and ushered them in.

Rance collapsed on the nearest pile of hay and Angie immediately took charge. 'I need to see to his wounds, Thomas. Will you keep guard for us?'

'Be proud to, ma'am. I've got a fine new Winchester to keep me company. Yours is under the hay next to you, Mr Rance.'

The sight of the gleaming new weapon served to take away some of the pain as Angie began to investigate his injuries. It transpired that the lawman had been uncommonly lucky. Both were flesh wounds, the bullets having passed clean through without apparently leaving any infected pieces of clothing inside. Gangrene was a mortal terror, often far more dangerous than the bullet itself.

Planning ahead, Thomas had thought

to provide a clean shirt. Briskly tearing this into sections, Angie cleaned off and bandaged both wounds. 'You're going to have to keep off that leg for a while,' she stated matter-of-factly. 'If you want it to heal, that is.'

'What I want it to do is hold my weight,' replied Rance firmly. 'This thing isn't finished yet.' He placed his bloodstained hands over hers and stared deep into her eyes. 'I need you to stop or at least slow the bleeding down so that I can get around. Please!'

Before she could reply to that, there was an urgent cry from the stablehand. 'We've got visitors, Mr Rance. Three looks like. Only one of them's staying well back.'

'That'll be Bodeen. He makes a habit of that. How's about you picking one of them off?'

'It's years since I done shot me a white man,' responded Thomas in all seriousness. Then his face creased into a smile again as he continued, 'No offence to you folks of course.'

'None taken, Thomas,' replied Rance. 'And aim low. Just so as you bring him down.'

As Angie tied a tourniquet around his leg, Rance watched Thomas slide the powerful rifle through a chink in the door. Sighting carefully down the twenty-four-inch barrel, the man inhaled, then slowly exhaled and squeezed the trigger. With all three men backlit by such a spectacular blaze, he really couldn't miss.

* * *

As the two reluctant point men came level with the bank, there was a loud report over at the livery and one of them slewed sideways. As the luckless gunman tumbled to the ground, his head struck the timber boardwalk and he lay still. It was all too much for his companion. Without so much as a glance at his leader, he abruptly turned down the side of the bank building and ran as though the hounds of hell were after him. At any other time Bodeen would have gunned him down from behind as a lesson to others, but he now had far more pressing business. For the first time since riding into Devil's Lake he was actually outnumbered.

16

'I'm coming for you, Bodeen, you black-hearted son of a bitch. You're a dead man!'

Rance Toller had limped over to the main entrance, so as to make his intentions known. The bleeding from his leg had slowed, but what he really needed was rest. Angie regarded him sadly, knowing that he was not likely to get any of that for a while.

In some ways, she reflected, he was very like the man that he now intended to pursue. Both could kill without compunction. Both were entirely ruthless, although in Bodeen's case it was gratuitous. It would doubtless be held against Rance that he had almost single-handedly destroyed much of the town that he was sworn to protect. Then again, the good citizens of Devil's Lake had effectively withdrawn their support from him when they made a compact with the mining speculators, which in turn had directly brought on the death of her husband.

My God, she mused, is it only three days since he was gunned down in front of me?

Shaking her head, she watched the town marshal as he checked over his new Winchester. For all his faults, she couldn't imagine parting from him after all this was over — if he survived. Suddenly she felt his eyes on her. Holding his intense gaze, she smiled.

When he finally spoke, his tone was deadly serious. 'You've got to promise me that whatever happens out there, you won't come after me. Bodeen is temporarily without an army, so you'll easily be able to get away. I mean it, Angie. I want your word.'

Reluctantly she complied, but he did just wonder if you could ever really trust a woman. Somehow, the concept of shaking on a deal done didn't ring true with a female.

Thomas temporarily pulled his attention off the street and doubtfully contemplated Rance. Somehow the marshal looked just a bit too beaten up to be street fighting with a professional killer. Nevertheless, he dutifully made his report. 'Bodeen headed off behind the back of the telegraph office, Marshal.'

That made sense. There were far more buildings to use for concealment on that side of town. Rance nodded as he headed for the livery's rear door. 'Keep an eye out for any movement. If you see anything, just holler out and you can be sure I'll hear. You won't need no two hollers!'

With that, he carefully opened the small door and eased out. The gunshot rang out before he was even clear of the entrance. Dropping to the ground, he winced as a sharp pain lanced through his right leg. Just where had that come from?

He didn't have to wait long to find out. From well beyond the town, shouting broke out and there was another shot. The battered regulator who had turned tail and run was busy stealing a horse from the good citizens assembled over yonder.

Despite his discomfort, Rance chuckled. There was just no escaping the grief that they had brought on themselves. Calling back to Angie that he was unhurt, Rance struggled to his feet. Keeping his back to the livery, he moved carefully around the building. Every sense was alert. It was just him and Bodeen, and he now had a rifle that could certainly match the Sharps in a restricted area. With every step, he crunched through crusted snow. Surely the man must hear such progress, he considered ruefully.

Finally the lawman, for he still considered himself to be one, reached the corner of the building. Now was the time of greatest danger. Any movement into the open could bring an instantaneous reaction. It was a sad reality that if he was now the hunter, then the first move had to be his and he really was feeling well used. Did he run or crawl? With a throbbing leg wound, neither prospect appealed. Yet the thought of crawling slowly and painfully through hard snow settled it for him. Gripping his rifle, he drew in a deep breath and prepared to run.

The gunshot came from off to his left, near the livery entrance. It was followed by another, and another. The window of the telegraph office had completely disintegrated. Then he heard a door slam. Unable to contain himself, Rance risked a quick look down the front of the building. By Christ, Angie was sprinting for the boardwalk further up the street. She was obviously going for position. So much for a woman's promise!

* * *

Angie watched Rance slip out of the rear door. The sudden gunshot sent her heart into her mouth. Even though he

253

quickly called to say that he was unhurt, her mind was made up. Whatever meaningless oath she had just muttered meant nothing to her. Along with Thomas, there were three of them and only one of Bodeen. The odds were never likely to be that favourable again.

'Thomas,' she called softly, 'what say we all of us hunt down that murderous son of a bitch? Rance is all set to get himself killed out there, with that gammy leg and all.'

The stablehand regarded her warmly. It was mighty obvious that she held feelings for the marshal. She also had grit *and* she was right. If he remained unaided, the odds were definitely against the lawman. Mind made up he replied, 'I ain't got the wind that I used to; you'll have to run whilst I cover.'

* * *

Bodeen had forced the rear door of the telegraph office and had made his way through to the front. Like all the buildings in Devil's Lake that morning it was empty. Its citizens were just like so many sheep. Bark at them and they all ran. Staying back from the window, he kneeled down and lined his Sharps on the livery. The slight distortion of the glass was annoying, but smashing it would only give his position away. He had no doubt that Marshal Toller would soon show himself. That poor dumb son of a bitch just never knew when to back off. And for what, $75 a month and found? Hell, a man could earn more than that in a single day just by holding up a stagecoach. Even better, if you had somebody else do it and just took a cut, then you didn't even risk getting shot at.

The window before him shattered abruptly and a splinter nicked his already disfigured face. Flinching from the pain, he backed away slightly. The shot had come from the livery entrance and was soon followed by more. Even as the broken glass was falling out of its frame, Bodeen recognized the high-powered rifle as one that had belonged to his men. Then he saw the Sutter bitch burst out of the building and head off up the street. By Christ, they were trying to flank him!

* * *

However much Rance disliked Angie putting herself at risk, he had to acknowledge that the sudden intervention changed things. The covering fire could only have come from Thomas, which meant that there were now three of them actively in the fight. Steeling himself against the pain, he launched himself away from the livery and ran for the telegraph office. It was more of a stagger, but he made it without coming under fire. Thumping up against the timber wall, he allowed himself to drop down to its base. From inside there came muffled cursing and then a single heavy calibre bullet punched through the boarding.

Thinking rapidly, Rance bellowed out, 'Better say your prayers, Bodeen. There's a stick of dynamite coming through with your name on it.'

Heavy footsteps sounded in the office and then a crash, followed by gunfire from over by the bank.

★ ★ ★

Angie's chest was heaving as she dropped down next to the boardwalk outside the town's only bank. Thomas's burst of rapid fire had obviously worked, because her frantic dash had not attracted Bodeen's malevolent attention. She was safely situated in time to witness Rance's ungainly sprint over to the telegraph office. His collapse by the wall was followed by a loud report from inside. Tucking the Henry into her shoulder, she desperately searched for a target. Then a holler came from Rance that she couldn't quite catch, but it seemed to include the word dynamite.

The rear door of the telegraph office burst open with tremendous force. Instinctively she opened fire. As the bullet struck the door, she levered another cartridge in just as Bodeen appeared at the run. Instinctively she snapped off another shot. Her spirits soared as she saw him jerk under the impact of her bullet and fall on to his right side. Reloading, she screamed out, 'I've hit him, I've hit him!'

She frenziedly tried to line up another shot, but somehow he'd just managed to crawl out of sight. Looking over to where Rance was back on his feet, she bawled, 'He's on the run!'

The lawman smiled grimly as he clambered painfully to his feet. His little ploy had worked. Between them they now had to either bring Bodeen down or at least keep him on the move. The self-styled regulator was being hunted down like a wounded timber wolf. Edging cautiously round to the rear of the telegraph office, he spotted fresh blood in the snow.

'Good girl, Angie,' he muttered.

At that moment she appeared on his left flank. Silently, he indicated that she should move up the main street and then sweep down the next alley. They had to keep the pressure on.

* * *

Agony coursed through his left shoulder. The bullet was lodged deep against the joint. It would require a sawbones to get it out. The whole left side of his body was greasy with blood. Only sheer cussedness had enabled Bodeen to regain his feet and keep moving. For some reason he headed for the north end of town, back towards the flames. Still clutching the Truthful Sharps and grinding his teeth against the intense pain, he staggered on. He couldn't hear anyone following, but he knew that they were there.

* * *

Thomas cautiously left the livery building. The new rifle felt good in his hands. It had been fifteen years since he had last used one in anger, serving his new masters as a Yankee soldier. Slowly he crossed the deserted street, all the time searching for any sign of life. This really wasn't his fight, but something about Bodeen's bullying, domineering character had triggered bad memories from his past. The former slave didn't just want to hear about the Southerner's death, he wanted to see it.

★　★　★

Rance Toller and Dan Bodeen spotted each other at the same instant. They were both at the rear of the dry goods store, one at each end of the building. Both raised their rifles, took rapid aim and fired. Bodeen was marginally faster in getting his shot off, but he just couldn't keep his left arm steady and the heavy bullet slammed into a section of wood cladding. In Rance's case, his side wound pulled his aim to the left so that his projectile passed by his enemy at waist height. Fuming with frustration, Bodeen then did the unthinkable: he dropped his cherished single shot Sharps rifle into the slush, turned away and ran.

Cursing his poor marksmanship, Rance levered in another cartridge. He couldn't believe the direction that his foe was taking: the regulator was heading for the alley between Pearsall's and the hotel. Yet that area was now a sea of flame. The fire had spread over to the saloon, so that part of the large structure was also on fire. Then the marshal remembered: his Winchester and two others lay in that alley, along with a couple of corpses.

* * *

As Bodeen approached the alley the heat became unbearable. Yet without a repeating rifle he couldn't hope to hold off the stinking jackals following hard on his heels. Pulling the collar of the heavy coat up around his ears, he plunged into the opening. Steam came from his clothing. He could feel the hair on his head singeing. He was in the midst of a firestorm and he was going to die. Then his right foot stubbed into a hard object. Reaching down, he grabbed the barrel and forestock of a Winchester and screamed. The heat from the metal burned into his unprotected hand but he would not let go. Struggling past the scorched bodies of his men to the other end of the narrow lane, he flung himself well out into the main street and dropped to his knees in the mud. Cradling the rifle in his left arm, Bodeen plunged his tormented flesh into a pool of melted snow.

Angie Sutter found him like that as she crept along the boardwalk in front of the dry goods store. With his broad back to her, she had no idea what he was up to, nor did she care. The man before her had shot down her husband in a very similar position only three days earlier, but at much greater range. Her kill was going to be far easier. Slowly and deliberately, she sighted down the barrel of her rifle. She was so close that the foresight seemed to be almost resting on his body. Such was her intensity that the roaring fire and groaning of timbers faded into the background. Her finger tightened on the trigger and then she just froze. Despite her fervent desire for vengeance, Angie just couldn't do it.

Some sixth sense alerted Bodeen to her presence. Ignoring the unremitting pain in his right hand, he took hold of the Winchester and shifted in the mud, so that he was suddenly presenting his left side to her. He sized up the situation in an instant and a leer spread to his awfully burnt features.

'You just ain't got the *cojones* have you, missy?'

A loud gunshot crashed out some little distance behind her and the top of

Bodeen's head appeared to lift off in a welter of blood and brain matter. As if in a dream, she heard the working of a lever action and then there was another detonation. A second bullet caught Bodeen in the torso and this was rapidly followed by a third. Only at that point, with her tormentor sprawled lifeless in the mud, did she slowly turn around. It was then that Rance, holding a smoking long gun, chose to answer Bodeen's question.

'Maybe not, but she's got one thing that you haven't. Decency!'

The two of them, the bloodied and battered but ultimately unbowed town marshal and his very attractive deputy, regarded each other in contemplative silence for some moments. Then with a broad smile Rance remarked, 'Looks like the local law had the edge on those regulators!'

Such was their absorption in each other that neither of them spotted the Spencer repeating carbine as it appeared over the false front of the dry goods store. Slowly it lined up on the unsuspecting figure of Marshal Toller. The face of its owner wore an expression of undiluted hatred. Yet he was so intent on his deadly purpose that he failed to notice his own impending doom.

The single gunshot followed by a heavy thump took everybody by surprise. Rance and Angie whirled around, rifles at the ready. A little way down the street stood Thomas, a smoking Winchester in his hands. Directly in front of the couple, embedded in the mud was Rance's missing Spencer. Stepping off the boardwalk, the lawman peered up at the false front. Jed, the saloonkeeper, lay slumped on the edge of it. Blood trickled over the hoarding. The man was quite obviously very dead.

Thomas grinned. 'That man should have stuck to tending bar, Mr Rance,' he remarked. Then he burst into an overly loud fit of laughter. It held an edge of hysteria that suggested great discomfort at having killed a fellow human being.

Rance limped over to join him. Reaching out, he took the other man's right hand firmly in his. 'You did just fine, Thomas. Just fine. Now there's one last thing I would ask of you. There's a mighty big fire here that needs fighting. I'd take it kindly if you'd let those sorry-looking citizens know that the killing's over.'

The stablehand willingly agreed to the request, which of course served more than one purpose. Activity would act as a balm to the anguish that he was feeling over his first act of violence in many years. Like a bit player in a theatrical play, Thomas strode away purposefully leaving Rance and Angie to their thoughts. The marshal retrieved the unfired Spencer and then the two of them backed well away from the conflagration's relentless advance.

Angie had only one question. 'Why did that saloonkeeper take against you so?'

With the cessation of bloodshed, Rance felt a crushing fatigue beginning to overwhelm him. All he wanted to do was sleep. Favouring her with a tired smile, he replied, 'Guess I rode him too hard yesterday. Some men will take it and then back shoot you the first chance they get. Then again, maybe he just didn't like that I'd burned down his life's work and put him out of a job.'

Angie stared at him open-mouthed. He had uttered that without any apparent sign of humour. His chillingly ruthless approach to life again bore a startling similarity to that of the man lying in the mud not twenty yards away. The question was, could she tolerate that permanently?

17

Mister Rance Toller and Mrs Angie Sutter sat their horses outside the livery and looked up the length of Main Street. It was two days since the momentous confrontation had taken place. Christmas Day had come and gone with only scant acknowledgement. With the absence of any threat, there was a deal of activity on the thorough-fare, but it was noticeable that everybody studiously avoided eye contact with the two of them.

Despite the cold, the ashy remains of four buildings were still smoking. A pall of death seemed to hang over Devil's Lake, as though the water's mythical monsters and spirits had come to extract a deadly toll. The flesh of the many individuals who had been cremated in those structures had unpleasantly tainted the air. Sadly they weren't all hired guns.

To Rance's certain knowledge, a much-abused lady of ill repute had met her end in Pearsall's Emporium. The fire had finally been brought under control by the use of a fire-break. This had meant using some more of Silas Breckinridge's dynamite to level the dry goods store. Its owner had pleaded long and hard against such action, but it had to be. Either that or the flames would have claimed it in any case on the way to the next building.

'This should do you, folks,' proclaimed Thomas, as he appeared from the livery with two sacks of oats. His role in the final showdown was unknown to the townsfolk and he intended to keep it that way.

Angie accepted the feed with thanks and hung them behind her saddle. The mounted couple were about to undertake a journey, one that would take them a considerable distance from Devil's Lake. They had both agreed that there was no longer anything for them in Dakota Territory. Whatever negotiations took place between the town's citizens and big business held no interest for Rance. At best he would be left quietly alone, but the more likely scenario was that he would become a target for the kin of the many men who had perished in the conflict. As for Angie, she just wanted to be as far removed as possible from the dreadful events that had befallen her.

Rance leaned down cautiously from the saddle to take Thomas's hand. The wound in his side was healing but still very tender. 'You've been an unexpected friend, Thomas,' he remarked earnestly. 'We shall miss you.'

That individual had the good grace to appear slightly embarrassed and so looked down at his feet for a second. However, when he looked up again, his features registered honest interest.

'Are you going to settle an old fieldhand's curiosity and tell me where you're headed?'

'Well I reckon you can keep a secret,' replied Rance. 'We've both had enough of cold and snow. We're going south to Arizona. I've heard tell there's a nice town down there that welcomes industrious folk like us. Goes by the name of Tombstone. Sounds kind of quiet, don't it?'

THE END

We do hope that you have enjoyed reading this large print book.

Did you know that all of our titles are available for purchase?

We publish a wide range of high quality large print books including:
**Romances, Mysteries, Classics
General Fiction
Non Fiction and Westerns**

Special interest titles available in large print are:
**The Little Oxford Dictionary
Music Book, Song Book
Hymn Book, Service Book**

Also available from us courtesy of Oxford University Press:
**Young Readers' Dictionary
(large print edition)
Young Readers' Thesaurus
(large print edition)**

For further information or a free brochure, please contact us at:
**Ulverscroft Large Print Books Ltd.,
The Green, Bradgate Road, Anstey,
Leicester, LE7 7FU, England.
Tel:** (00 44) **0116 236 4325
Fax:** (00 44) **0116 234 0205**

TRAIL TO THE CAZADORES

Mark Bannerman

The five men who set out into the desert, searching for Joe Hennessey's wayward daughter, are bound together by very different motives: from greed for the offered reward to compassion for the young woman. But after an Indian attack results in the loss of his companions — plus his horse and gun — Texas Ranger Duncan is alone. Astray in this vast, hostile terrain, he is wounded and afraid. To top it all, the Indians who took his compatriots may soon return to take his scalp . . .